Jerry D

SHOELUX KIDS
Bible Stories

BOOK 6

Pacific Press® Publishing Association
Nampa, Idaho
Oshawa, Ontario, Canada
www.pacificpress.com

Designed by Dennis Ferree
Cover illustration by Kim Justinen
Inside illustrations by Mark Ford

Additional copies of this book may be purchased at
http://www.adventistbookcenter.com

ISBN: 0-8163-2005-5

03 04 05 06 07 • 5 4 3 2 1

CONTENTS

BIBLE STORY ADVENTURES

FOR KIDS:

The Bible is full of stories from long ago. And while it's fun to learn about the people and the places, it's also important to see how what the Bible says affects the way we live today—especially if we are trying to be friends of Jesus.

Shoebox Kids Bible Stories help you do both. Every chapter is a double story—first, a story from the Bible, then a story from today that shows one of the lessons that Bible story can teach us. That story—with *The Shoebox Kids*—is about learning what the Bible really means—at home, at school, or on the playground.

Every story is an adventure in learning to be more like Jesus!

FOR PARENTS AND TEACHERS:

Shoebox Kids Bible Stories does more than just give children information about the Bible—it shows them how to apply that information to everyday life. Teaching our children means going beyond information and entertainment to helping them learn to apply Bible truths. Too many of us grew up learning about the Bible, but not getting to know God. We can help the children we love by showing them not just what the Bible says, but what difference it makes in the way we live and love others.

Every Bible story has many lessons to teach and The Shoebox Kids story can teach only one of those. There may be others you can help your child learn.

The "Questions" at the end of each story can help you see what your child or children understand and what they may be confused about. Many of the questions can be discussion-starters that will help you understand the children you love better. They can help open the doors of communication, which are so important to reassuring them of your love and teaching them about God's.

Jerry D. Thomas

MEET THE SHOEBOX KIDS!

The Shoebox Kids are six friends who go to the same church. Their Sabbath School class meets in a really small room in the church. It's so small, everyone called it "the Shoebox." And their teacher's name is Mrs. Shue (you pronounce it just like "shoe"). So everyone calls them the Shoebox Kids.

Maria and Chris Vargas are Shoebox Kids. They live with their mom and dad and their little sister, Yolanda (everyone calls her Yoyo). Maria is in the fourth grade; Chris is in the third grade. They both are in the same classroom at their small church school.

Jenny Wallace is a Shoebox Kid. Her parents are divorced and she lives with her mother and her cat, Butterscotch. Her father lives nearby and she spends many weekends with him. She's in the fourth grade at the local public school.

Sammy Tan is a Shoebox Kid. He lives with his grandparents and is in the fourth grade in the church school. His parents were killed in a car crash when he was very young. He has one uncle.

Willie Teller is a Shoebox Kid. He lives with his parents and his dog, Coco. Willie is handicapped and wheels around in a cool wheelchair. He's in the fourth grade at the same public school as Jenny, but they're not in the same classroom.

DeeDee Adams is a Shoebox Kid. She lives with her parents and her older sister. She's in the third grade at the church school with Chris, Maria, and Sammy.

The Shoebox Kids live in Mill Valley, but they visit a lot of other interesting places. As they study their Bible lesson each week, they find that God is helping them learn about being His friend and treating others like Jesus did.

HIDING THE KING
Jesus' Hands

After Elisha died, the kings of Israel were just as wicked as King Ahab had been. Some of the kings of Judah were wicked also. King Jehoram married Athaliah, who was Ahab and Jezebel's daughter. When he was killed, their son Ahaziah was made king. He had learned from his mother to worship idols, so he was an evil king also.

When Ahaziah died, his mother decided that she would rule the country. She killed everyone who was related to Ahaziah—even her own grandchildren!

But Jehosheba, the wife of the high priest Jehoiada, heard what Athaliah was planning. She sneaked into the palace and took her nephew, baby Joash, and his nurse to a safe place. Aunt Jehosheba hid them safely in the temple for six years.

When Joash was seven years old, Jehoiada decided it was time to make him king. He told the other priests and temple workers, "Joash is alive!" Then he told them his plan. "You must bring all the leaders of the families of Israel to the temple. Then we will bring Joash out and announce that he is the new king. But you must protect him from Queen Athaliah."

HIDING THE KING

So Jehoiada brought Joash out to the front of the temple. He put the crown on Joash's head and the book of God's law in his hands. "Long live the king!" the people shouted. The priests and temple workers surrounded Joash with their spears and swords to keep him safe.

When Queen Athaliah heard the shouting, she came running to the temple. But Jehoiada commanded his men to arrest her and take her away. Even though he was only seven years old, Joash was the new king of Judah!

For many years, the rulers of Israel had been evil. Altars to worship idols had been built in many places. And many of the nice things from God's temple had been stolen. But Jehoiada had taught Joash to follow God, and Joash wanted his people to worship God again. So the people tore down many of the altars and came to the temple again.

When he was older, Joash could see that God's temple didn't look very good. It needed to be repaired, and many of the stolen things needed to be replaced. But there wasn't enough money to fix everything. So Joash made a special box and placed it near the temple door. Then he asked the people to give offerings of money to God. "Please give so that we can make God's house look beautiful again."

And the people did give. They gave so much money that the box filled up. Joash had enough money to hire workers to repair the temple and build new furniture to replace the things that had been stolen.

For many years Joash was a good king who followed God. But after Jehoiada died, Joash forgot about God. He worshiped idols and stopped going to the temple.

He wouldn't listen to God's prophet, Zechariah. He got so mad that he had Zechariah killed. In fact, he turned into such a bad king that one day his servants killed him.

It was a very sad ending for a boy who started out being such a good king and such a good follower of God.

Jesus' Hands

"**W**oooh, wooh, wooh, whaa!"

Sammy Tan rolled over on his bed and groaned. "I wish that dog would go back to sleep," he mumbled. He barely opened his eyes, but he saw a red light flash through his window.

"Woooh, Whaa!"

This time the sound was louder. "Hey, that's no dog," Sammy said as he jumped up out of his bed and ran to open his window. "That's a fire truck!" The wail of the siren sounded close.

With the breeze coming in, Sammy smelled smoke. When he twisted his neck to look down his street, he saw flames on the roof of the third house down. In a flash, he was out of his room and down the hall to the living room. His grandmother was standing there with the front door open. "Grandmother, the Tashers' house is on fire!" he exclaimed as he stepped out onto the porch.

"Yes," she answered sadly, and then the fire truck went roaring by. "Come in and get your shoes on, Sammy," she called to him. "Grandfather wants to go help if we can." He nodded at her and ran back to grab his sneakers. Soon the three of them walked quickly across the lawns toward the flashing lights and shouting firemen.

"I hope the Tashers got out safely," Grandfather said. Sammy's mouth fell open. He was so interested in the truck and the fire that he hadn't thought about the people who lived there. Little Tommy and Tony Tasher were too young to be friends of his, but suddenly he was worried about them.

"Let's hurry," Sammy said and started to run.

"Sammy, slow down," his grandfather said. "The firemen are in charge of getting people out. We'll stay back out of their way unless they ask for our help."

Sammy could see the firemen rushing back and forth, aiming their big hoses at the fire. When he saw a fireman leading the whole Tasher family around the side of the house, Sammy cheered.

"There they are! They're safe!" he shouted and pointed. The fireman brought them across the yard to where Sammy and his family were standing.

"Would you stay with them here for a few minutes?" the fireman asked Sammy's grandmother. She nodded and put her arm around Mrs. Tasher.

"Where's Boots?" Tony suddenly asked. "I want Boots."

"It's our dog," Mr. Tasher explained to the fireman. "He's tied up in the backyard."

"I'll go get him, now, son," the fireman said to Tony. Then he disappeared around the house.

Mrs. Tasher shivered as she watched the firemen spraying the flames on her roof. "You're getting chilled out here," Sammy's grandmother said to the Tashers. "Would you like to go to our house and be comfortable?"

"No, I think we should stay here," Mrs. Tasher answered.

"Grandmother?" Sammy spoke up. "I could run and get the blankets from the hall closet."

"Yes. Go, Sammy."

When he got back with the blankets, Sammy was glad to see that Tony had his arms around Boots. By now, only smoke was rising from the house, and the firemen were winding up some of the hoses. Mr. Tasher spoke to the fire chief for a few minutes and then came back to his family huddled under Sammy's blankets.

"Well, now we know why smoke alarms are so important." He hugged Tony and Boots. "At least we're all safe. The fire chief says we can come back in the morning. Tonight, we'll go to a hotel."

"But what about Boots?" Tony cried out. "He has to stay with us now."

Sammy saw that Mr. Tasher didn't know what to do. He knew that dogs weren't usually allowed in hotel rooms. He knelt down beside Tony. "How about if Boots stays in my backyard tonight? He'd be safe there, and when you come back in the morning, you can run right over and get him."

Mr. Tasher looked at Sammy's grandfather, who nodded and smiled. Then he spoke to Sammy. "That's very kind of you, Sammy. I think Boots will like that, don't you, Tony?"

Tony looked at Sammy and smiled, too. "I know Boots will like it." Then he handed the little white dog to Sammy and followed his mother to a car.

Sammy's grandmother put her arm around him as they walked home.

The next morning, in the Shoebox, Sammy looked tired but happy. He told his friends about the fire and the hoses and Boots and everything. Later, his eyes kept trying to close while Mrs. Shue talked about Joash and how he did God's work even though he was just a kid. Then Mrs. Shue did something that got Sammy's attention.

"Sammy, come up here please. Hold your hand up on this poster board." Sammy spread his fingers against the thick paper and watched Mrs. Shue trace around them with a pencil.

"Thank you, Sammy," Mrs. Shue said, as she took her scissors with the orange handles and cut along the pencil line. "This quarter, I want you to remember that even though you are young, Jesus has work He wants you to do. In fact," she said as she cut, "Jesus wants you to be His hands in this world."

She held up the cut-out picture of Sammy's hand. As she walked to the front wall, Sammy noticed for the first time that a blanket covered most of it. Mrs. Shue reached up and pulled the blanket away.

There, attached to the wall in a dozen different ways, was the strangest collection the Shoebox Kids had ever seen. There were gloves of every kind hanging there on the wall.

"Look," Chris laughed, "there's a baseball mitt and a boxing glove."

"And a big leather glove and a mitten," Jenny added.

"There are many different kinds of gloves because there are many different ways to do Jesus' work. Sammy, I wanted to trace your hand first because you did Jesus' work last night."

"I did?" Sammy was confused. "But I didn't preach or even tell the Tashers about Jesus."

Mrs. Shue just smiled. "Sammy, what do you think Jesus

would have done if He had been there last night at the fire?"

"I guess He would have tried to help the Tashers any way He could. He would have been extra nice to them."

"And that's just what you did, Sammy. You got blankets for them, and you were extra nice to Tony when you offered to keep his dog. You did what Jesus would have done. You were Jesus' hands."

Sammy stared at his own two hands and then at the gloves on the wall. It was hard to believe. "I guess you're right," he said at last.

"Then take this cut-out of your hand and slip it into one of the gloves on our wall. Choose whatever glove you think best shows the work you did for Jesus."

Sammy stared at the wall while Mrs. Shue continued. "This quarter, I want you all to watch for chances to be Jesus' hands. And when you do some work for Him, you can cut out a hand print and slip it into a glove on the wall."

Sammy stepped up and slid his paper hand into a fireman's heavy rubber glove. "Being Jesus' hands at a fire was really exciting. I hope I can do something else for Him soon."

The rest of the Shoebox Kids hoped they could, too.

QUESTIONS

1. Does your house have smoke alarms? Ask a parent to be sure the alarms are working properly.

2. Did you know that anytime you are kind to others, you are doing Jesus' work?

3. Has Jesus ever used your hands to do His work? Will you be His hands this quarter?

CHAPTER

WHEN THE SUN MOVED BACKWARD
Big Teeth

As the years went by in Judah and Israel, some kings followed God and some worshiped idols. Finally, God allowed the Assyrians to conquer Israel. They took the people of Israel to Assyria as captives. But Ahaz, the king of Judah was evil also. He took the furniture out of God's temple and led his people in worshiping idols. Would God allow an army to conquer Judah also?

When Ahaz died, his son Hezekiah became king. Unlike his father, Hezekiah wanted to follow God. He told the priests to clean the temple and build new furniture. Then Hezekiah worshiped there to show everyone in the city that he wanted to follow God.

But Hezekiah wanted the whole country to follow God. He invited everyone in Judah and those who were still left in Israel to come and celebrate the Passover Feast at the temple in Jerusalem. The people came and were happy to worship God again. When they went home, they tore down the altars of the idols.

Before long, the Assyrians attacked Judah also. Sennacherib (Sen-nak-er-ib), the king of Assyria, captured many cities. Hezekiah didn't want his people to be taken captive, so he gave Sennacherib all the silver and gold from the palace and the temple, hoping the Assyrians would go away.

But they didn't go away. King Sennacherib told the people of Judah, "You can't trust anyone to protect you. Your king says that your God will save you from me, but He can't. Your king is only fooling you."

Hezekiah prayed. "Help us, God. The Assyrians have defeated many other countries and destroyed their gods. But they cannot defeat You. Show the world Your power and save us!"

God answered Hezekiah's prayer. He sent an angel to destroy Sennacherib's whole army. By the next morning, every Assyrian soldier was dead. God wasn't fooling His people. He saved them just as Hezekiah had promised.

Some years later, Hezekiah got very sick. When he was nearly dead, the prophet Isaiah came to the palace to visit him. "What does God say?" he asked Isaiah. "Will I get well?"

Isaiah shook his head. "No, God says you will not get well. Give everyone your last orders. You will die."

King Hezekiah turned his head and stared out the palace window. He could see the shadow of the afternoon sun climbing up the palace steps as it did every day. He prayed, "God, please make me well. Remember that I have always served You and done what was right."

Isaiah was still walking out through the palace when God spoke to him. "Go back to Hezekiah and tell him, 'I will heal you. You will live fifteen more years.' "

When Hezekiah heard this, he was very happy. But he wanted to be sure. "What sign can you give me that God will heal me?" he asked Isaiah.

"Look out the window," Isaiah answered. "Watch the shadow of the sun on the steps." Hezekiah watched. Instead of going up the steps, the shadow started moving *down!* The sun was moving backward in the sky!

When Hezekiah saw the sun moving backward in the sky, he knew that he would get well and live for fifteen more years. He knew he could trust God to take care of him.

Big Teeth

"**W**oof! Grrrr."

Jenny was halfway across her yard, headed toward the car where her mother sat waiting. But that sound told her that the Thompsons' big dog, Fang, was loose again and in her yard. And Jenny was afraid.

"Come on, Jenny," Mrs. Wallace called from the car.

Jenny twisted her head around and saw the big black dog's mean eyes staring right at her. And she saw his big teeth.

Jenny closed her eyes, took a deep breath, then turned and ran for her life toward the car. Sure that the dog's teeth were right behind her, she jerked the door open and jumped in.

"Jenny, why are you so afraid of dogs? You've never been bitten by one." Mrs. Wallace asked as Jenny buckled her seat belt.

"I don't know, Mom. They have such big teeth. I get scared just thinking about them." Jenny shivered as she talked.

Later, in the Shoebox, Mrs. Shue made an announcement. "Our Mill Valley Fire and Police Department is asking for our help. Sometimes, when there is an emergency, like a fire or car accident, children get hurt or scared."

Sammy spoke up. "Like when Tony and Tommy Tasher's house caught on fire last week."

"That's right, Sammy," Mrs. Shue agreed. "When firefighters or officers see hurt or scared children, they try to help them feel better. One way they can do that is by giving them a gift."

"I always feel better when I get presents," Willie said.

"We all do," Mrs. Shue laughed. "So the people at the police and fire departments are asking us to donate stuffed animals, like teddy bears, for them to give away. They would like any old stuffed animals that you don't play with anymore."

There was a buzz in the room while everyone talked at the same time about their stuffed animals. When they settled down again, the Shoebox Kids had agreed to donate four teddy bears, two dogs, a cat, a horse, and a lizard.

"Where did you ever find a stuffed lizard?" Jenny asked Chris.

"He was hiding under a stuffed rock!" Chris answered. Everyone laughed.

DeeDee raised her hand. "Mrs. Shue, can we collect more animals? I'm sure the police need more than just a few."

"Yes, you can, DeeDee. The police department sent us these information letters in case you wanted to ask people in your neighborhood to donate animals also."

DeeDee whispered to Maria and Jenny, "Let's ask our mothers if we can go collecting stuffed animals tomorrow."

After church, their mothers agreed that it was a good idea. "They can go together to the houses in their neighborhoods," DeeDee's mother suggested.

"They can start in our neighborhood tomorrow," Jenny's mother added. "I'll be home then in case they need any help."

Jenny and Maria and DeeDee were excited to be able to do something for others, to be Jesus' hands, and to be able to have fun doing it together.

When they started out the next day, Jenny remembered Fang. DeeDee and Maria noticed that she was very quiet. "What's wrong, Jenny?" Maria asked. "Don't you want to collect more animals?"

"I want to," Jenny answered as she turned to look behind them. "I just don't want to go out in my neighborhood."

"Aren't your neighbors nice?" Maria asked.

"Oh, yes, the people are," Jenny answered, looking around carefully.

"What are you looking for?" DeeDee interrupted. "You keep looking around like you're afraid of something."

Jenny hung her head. "The Thompsons have a big black dog named Fang. I'm watching out for him because he scares me."

Maria looked around. She seemed a little frightened, too. "How big is he?" she asked in whispery voice.

"Wait a minute," DeeDee said. "My mother taught me how to deal with dogs. Let's go." She turned and started down the street. "You have to know that dogs always try to find out who's the toughest, who's dominant, when they meet. That's why you see them stare at each other and growl and show their teeth."

"Fang has big teeth," Jenny said with a shiver.

DeeDee went on. "Whenever you walk into a dog's yard, he sees you as a threat to his property. A dog that's used to being the toughest, wants to know if he's tougher than you. That's why you should not lean over and look him in the eye and smile."

"But doesn't that show that you're friendly?" Maria asked.

"Not to a dog," DeeDee said. "To him, you're doing everything but growling to prove that you are tougher, more dominant. So he wants to prove his toughness by fighting."

"So what should I do if a big dog runs at me?" Jenny asked.

"Just stand still. Don't run, don't scream, just stand still and straight. Let the dog come to you. Talk to it in a calm voice if you can. But let him decide that he is the toughest and you are no threat to him."

"Then he'll go away?"

"He'll walk away and you can back slowly out of his yard. If he runs at you again, just freeze again." DeeDee smiled at her friends. "It's not that bad. You get used to dealing with dogs after a while. And only a few are really mean."

The girls began knocking on doors, and the people were happy to help. Soon, each of the girls was carrying several stuffed animals. As they struggled toward the last house, DeeDee slipped and dropped her six teddy bears on the sidewalk. "Wait here," Jenny laughed, "and babysit my four monkeys. I'll go ask the Thompsons." She was almost to the door when she heard the growl.

There was Fang, right at the corner of the house, staring straight at her. Jenny stopped, and all she could think of was to pray. "Jesus, help me! Save me from this mean dog's teeth!"

Then Jenny remembered what DeeDee had said. She stood straight up and watched out of the corner of her eyes as Fang walked up to her, still growling and showing those teeth. Jenny just stood there. She even tried to talk to him. "That's a good boy, Fang." Fang stopped growling and looked confused.

Out on the sidewalk, DeeDee and Maria held their breath. Just then, the door of the house flew open. "Fang, come here. Leave that poor girl alone!" It was Mrs. Thompson. Immediately, Fang ran to her. "I'm sorry, Jenny."

Jenny started breathing again. She tried to smile. Mrs. Thompson went on. "Come on in. And bring your friends. Fang, you should be ashamed for being mean to these nice girls."

Fang did look ashamed. He crawled along the floor and tried to cover his sad eyes with his paws. Jenny almost felt sorry for him. "Why, he's just a big puppy," she said.

"Just a big baby," Mrs. Thompson agreed. "Fang, I want you to be friends with Jenny. Come here." Fang jumped up and walked over to Jenny and Mrs. Thompson. "Now,

Fang, shake hands and say you're sorry. Jenny, put your hand out."

Jenny hesitated, but she put her hand out toward Fang and his teeth. Fang raised his paw, and they shook. Then, he opened his mouth and . . . licked Jenny's hand twice. "Now you'll be friends," Mrs. Thompson said.

Jenny petted Fang while her friends explained about the stuffed animals. *Thank You, Jesus,* she prayed silently, *for helping me remember what to do out in the yard. Thank You for helping me make Fang my friend.*

QUESTIONS

1. Have you ever been afraid of big dogs?

2. Have you learned what to do if a strange dog runs at you?

3. Did Jesus do a miracle and protect Jenny? Could it be a miracle to help her remember what to do so she wouldn't be hurt?

4. Has Jesus ever done a miracle like that for you?

CHAPTER

JOSIAH AND THE LOST BOOK
The Big Cookie Mistake

After Hezekiah died, his son Manasseh became king. Manasseh was a bad king. He built back all the altars to idols that his father had torn down. He wrecked the temple and set up a place to worship idols inside. After fifty-five years, he died and his son Amon became king. Amon was just as bad as his father. He ruled for only two years before his own soldiers killed him.

Even though Amon's son Josiah was only eight years old, he was crowned king. Josiah was different from his father and grandfather. He was a good king like his ancestor David. He always did his best to follow God.

As he got older, Josiah ordered his soldiers to tear down the altars to idols in Jerusalem and in Judah. He hired carpenters, builders, and stone cutters to repair the temple once more. He wanted to teach his people to worship God in the temple again.

Hilkiah, the high priest, was in charge of all the workmen. As they worked, he cleaned out the old storage rooms. Inside, he found an old scroll. When he unrolled it, Hilkiah could hardly believe his eyes. It was the Book of the Law—the first books of the Bible written by Moses many years before!

Hilkiah took the scroll to Shaphan, King Josiah's royal assistant. "Look," he cried, "I found the Book of the Law!" Shaphan took the book to Josiah and read it to him.

Josiah had not heard the words of the Law at school. He had not heard them at home. He had never heard those words from God in his whole life. Now he heard how God wanted His people to live. Now he heard how God wanted His people to treat each other and how they could be happy. He heard all the promises God gave for those who loved Him and followed Him. Suddenly Josiah knew how far his people of Judah had grown away from God. He was so upset that he cried and tore his robe.

He sent messengers to God's prophetess, Huldah. "Ask God what we should do about the words in this book," he begged her. "I know God is angry with us because the people of Judah have not obeyed His words for many years. They didn't do the things they were supposed to do."

Huldah talked to God and gave His answer to Josiah. "The people of Judah don't follow Me anymore. All their idols have made Me angry. Now My anger toward them is like a fire that cannot be put out."

But God had a special message for Josiah. "Because you want to do the right thing and follow Me, you will have peace. I won't bring My anger against Judah until after you die."

Josiah called together all the leaders of Judah and Jerusalem and read God's words to them. "I will follow God's laws," he promised to everyone. Then he traveled around the country destroying the idols and the evil places of worship. He called all the people in the land together to celebrate Passover in Jerusalem again, just like God's law told them to do.

For thirty-one years, Josiah led his people to follow God and obey His word. He was one of the best kings Judah ever had.

The Big Cookie Mistake

The first thing Chris saw when they turned down the street toward home was the big moving truck. "Hey, look! Someone's moving into the Andersons' old house." His dad slowed down, and everyone stared at the men carrying boxes and furniture into the house.

"Can we go see who's moving in?" Maria asked.

"Change your church clothes first. Then you can go and say hello while I'm getting lunch on the table. Find out how many are in the family, and maybe tomorrow we can take over a dish," Mrs. Vargas said.

Chris and Maria and Yoyo changed in a hurry and raced down the street. Chris led the way to the front door and pushed the doorbell. *Ding-dong,* it rang with a cheery sound. They heard footsteps, and then the door opened.

"Hi!" It was a boy about Chris's age. The room behind him was filled with scattered furniture and boxes—some opened but full, some empty, and some still sealed closed. A woman's head appeared above one tall box. She smiled.

"Who is it, Ryan?" she called out.

Ryan said, "I don't know yet."

Chris laughed. "Hi! I'm Chris Vargas, and these are my sisters, Maria and Yoyo. We live down the street. We just wanted to see who was moving in."

Ryan's mother called out again. "Hi, kids. I wish we could invite you in to play, but we have a lot of unpacking to do today. Why don't you come by tomorrow and show Ryan around the neighborhood?"

"We will," Chris answered. "See you tomorrow."

Ryan followed them out the door. "Ryan, do you have any sisters?" Maria asked.

"No, I'm an only child. But I do have a dog named Columbus."

"That's nice," Maria said.

Back at home, Yoyo reported first. "Mom, you don't need to send them a dish tomorrow. They already have dishes. I saw them in a box."

Mrs. Vargas laughed. "Yoyo, I meant that I wanted to send them a dish of food, just to welcome them to our neighborhood." She hugged her little girl tight. "How many are in the family?"

"Just a boy, my age; his name is Ryan," Chris almost shouted.

"Well, he does have a mother, but no sisters at all," Maria reported unhappily.

"He's just a homely child," Yoyo added sadly.

They all stared at Yoyo. "What?" Mrs. Vargas asked.

"Ryan said it! He said he was a homely child!" Yoyo defended herself.

Chris laughed. "No, Yoyo. He said he was an *only* child. That's means he doesn't have any brothers or sisters. Mom, his mother invited us to come by tomorrow and show Ryan the neighborhood. May we?"

"That's a good plan. We'll make something for you to take to them when you go."

The Big Cookie Mistake

The next morning, Chris was in the kitchen, cooking for the first time in his life. He had convinced his mother that the best thing they could make for their new neighbors was chocolate-chip cookies. And then she convinced him that he could bake them.

"Here's the recipe," she said when most of the stuff was mixed together, "and here are the rest of the ingredients. Just dump the sugar and flour and baking soda in and stir it up good. Then spread it out in this pan and pop it into the oven. I'll turn the oven on now. Call me when it looks ready to take out." Then she left to do the laundry in the other room.

I like sweet cookies, Chris thought, *so I'll add some extra sugar and leave out some of the flour.* Then he reached for the baking soda. It looked funny. He tasted a little bit on his tongue. "Yuck! I'm not putting that stuff in my cookies." He mixed up the rest of the ingredients and soon had the cookies in the oven.

But the first time he opened the door to check on them, he knew something was wrong.

A few days later, Chris was at Ryan's house. They had spent all week exploring the neighborhood. Now, they were going back to the park to look for that squirrel's nest.

"Mom, can we take the last of the cookies?" Ryan asked.

"OK. Chris, be sure to thank your mother again for me for those delicious cookies. Be careful at the park."

They were sitting under a tree, waiting for the squirrel to show up when Ryan asked, "What are we going to do tomorrow?"

"I'm going to church," Chris answered.

Ryan just stared at him. "Do you like to go to church? My mom took me a few times, but I hated it. It was so boring!"

Chris smiled. "At my church, we have a special class for kids our age. We meet in our own room, called the Shoebox, and have a lot of fun. And we learn more about the Bible and about Jesus."

"That sounds like fun, but why would you want to know more about the Bible?" Ryan asked as he reached for the last cookie. "Isn't it just a lot of rules that tell you not to have fun?"

Chris took a deep breath. He wanted to say the right thing so Ryan would understand the Bible was important. Without closing his eyes, he prayed, *Jesus, please help me explain this to Ryan so that he wants to know more about You.* Then, seeing the cookie in Ryan's hand, he had an idea.

"Ryan, do you like these cookies?"

"Yes!" Ryan mumbled through a mouthful of cookies. "Peanut-butter cookies are my favorite."

"Well," Chris laughed, "you were supposed to be eating chocolate-chip cookies. And I was supposed to bake them."

"What happened?"

"Well, I didn't follow the recipe. I left out the things I thought would taste bad and put in extra sugar so they would taste even better. But when I put them in the oven, they just lay there and got as hard as bricks."

"Really?"

"They wouldn't break even if you dropped them. We had to throw them all in the trash. Then Mom made these peanut-butter cookies. She told me that if you want good cookies, you have to follow the recipe. But learning about the Bible is like baking cookies, you know?"

Ryan stopped chewing. "What do you mean?"

The Big Cookie Mistake

Chris went on. "The Bible is like a recipe for being happy. If you don't know what it says, you can't follow the recipe. And if you don't, you can mess up your life like I messed up those cookies."

Ryan thought about that until he swallowed. Then he said, "Could I go with you to your church sometime?"

Chris's face broke into a big smile. "Sure. How about tomorrow?"

"All right. No, I forgot. I'm going to see my dad this weekend. Is the next week OK?"

"Sure," Chris said. "There's the squirrel! Let's go."

The next day, in the Shoebox, Chris told the story of baking the cookies and talking to Ryan. "Next week, he'll be here."

Mrs. Shue nodded her head. "That's wonderful, Chris. You were certainly doing Jesus' work yesterday. Which glove do you want to fill when you make your hand cut-out?"

Chris pointed to the thick, blue, cook's glove. "I guess ruining those chocolate-chip cookies wasn't such a bad mistake after all."

QUESTIONS

1. Have you ever moved to a new house? Would you like someone like Chris and Maria to welcome you to a new neighborhood?

2. Have you ever baked cookies?

3. What did Chris do when he wasn't sure what to say to Ryan about the Bible?

4. Did you know that the Bible is a recipe for being happy?

5. Can you think of someone you could invite to church?

CHAPTER

SWALLOWED BY A FISH
Locked Out!

Jonah sat by the sea in the city of Joppa and stared out at the ships. He was thinking about the words God had spoken to him. "Go to Nineveh," God had said. "Preach to the people there and tell them that I don't like the evil things they are doing."

Jonah knew that the people of Nineveh were evil. Nineveh was a large city in Assyria, Israel's biggest enemy. Jonah shook his head. "I don't want to go to Nineveh. I'm afraid to tell my enemies what God has said. I'll run away instead."

So Jonah didn't go to Nineveh. He got on a boat that was going to Tarshish, a city very far away in the opposite direction from Nineveh. When the boat sailed away from the land and headed out to sea, Jonah let out a big sigh. "No one can find me now," he told himself as he lay down to sleep.

But God knew where Jonah was. He sent a strong wind that turned the sea into big waves. Before long, the ship was in danger. "This storm will soon tear our ship apart!" the captain shouted to his sailors. "Throw the cargo overboard! Maybe that will keep us from sinking."

But the storm only got worse. The sailors started praying to the gods they worshiped. "Save us!" they cried. But the wind got stronger and the waves got higher.

The captain saw Jonah lying under his coat. "Wake up!" he shouted. "We're all going to die if this ship sinks. Pray to your God. Maybe He will save us."

The sailors had another idea. "Let's roll lots (like dice) to see who is to blame for this storm." Back then, people used lots to try to decide what to do. Sometimes God controlled the lots to tell them what to do.

While the ship went up and down on the waves, the sailors rolled their lots—and Jonah's name was chosen. "I'm running away from God," he shouted to the sailors. "Throw me over the side, and your ship will be safe."

"No," the sailors shouted. "You'll drown." They tried to row the ship back to shore, but the storm got even worse. Finally, the sailors picked up Jonah and threw him over the side.

Splash! Jonah hit the water, and a big wave went over his head. But as he started to sink down, a big mouth opened up under him. A huge fish opened his mouth wide and swallowed Jonah!

Jonah sat in the fish's stomach for three days. He had time to think about what God wanted him to do. He had time to pray and ask God to forgive him for running away. So God had the fish spit Jonah out on the shore.

God said, "Now go to Nineveh and tell them what I told you."

So Jonah got up and walked to Nineveh. He went to the middle of the city and told the people that God knew about their evil ways. "In forty days, Nineveh will be destroyed," he shouted.

The people of Nineveh listened to Jonah. They repented and promised to stop doing evil things. Even the king was so sorry he tore off his robe and sat in ashes.

God was happy that they wanted to change. So He decided not to destroy Nineveh. But that didn't make Jonah happy. "I knew You would do this," Jonah said to God. "I knew You would forgive the people of Nineveh even though they are the enemies of Israel. That's why I didn't want to come here." Then he walked out of the city and sat down to pout.

While Jonah was sitting there trying to rest, God made a plant with big leaves grow very quickly beside him. Before long, Jonah was resting nicely in the shade. That made him happy.

But the next day, God sent a worm to eat the plant, and it died. Jonah sat in the sun, hot and unhappy. God spoke to him again. "You're unhappy that the plant died, even though you didn't plant it or take care of it. I created the people of Nineveh, and I love them. Can you understand why I don't want them to die?"

Then Jonah began to understand why God forgave the people of Nineveh instead of destroying the city.

Locked Out!

Click. Clack. Click. Clack.

"DeeDee, please stop pushing the buttons. It's driving me crazy," her mother said from the front seat.

"OK, Mother." DeeDee loved their new car. Every door could be locked or unlocked just by pushing the shiny buttons. She reached over and pushed a different button. *Bzzz.* Her window buzzed quietly down. *Bzzz.* It went back up. *Bzzz.* It came down again.

"DeeDee! Stop playing with the window. I know you like the new car, honey, but you can't play with it like it was a toy." They pulled up to DeeDee's school as her mother spoke. "Now, don't forget your lunch. And be sure to tell Mrs. Peterson that we can help her at the school Saturday night, but that your father is out of town."

"Yes, Mother. I will, Mother." DeeDee grabbed her books and ran into the building. Her Shoebox friends, Sammy and Maria, were at the drinking fountain.

"We have a new car!" DeeDee told them. "It's dark blue, and it's got power windows and everything."

"Is it here? Can we see it?" Maria asked, looking past DeeDee toward the door.

"No, but you can see it tomorrow at church. I can't wait to show you. You just push a button and 'click' the doors lock."

On the way home that afternoon, DeeDee started clicking the door locks again. "DeeDee, I've already asked you to stop doing that today. Have you forgotten?"

"No. I just like the way it sounds."

Mrs. Adams frowned. "I don't want you to play with those buttons anymore. You can lock or unlock the car when we get in or out, but otherwise, leave them alone. Do you understand?"

"Yes, Mother." DeeDee frowned, too. *I'm not hurting anything,* she thought. When they pulled into the driveway, she clicked the doors unlocked and didn't think about the buttons anymore that day.

The next morning, she was up early and anxious to get going. "Hurry, Mom. I don't want to be late," DeeDee called. There was no answer. "Mom?" Then she heard the front door close.

"It's chilly and starting to rain out there," her mother called out. "I started the car so it could warm up. Hurry now, DeeDee. I don't want to be late."

"Mom! I'm waiting for you," DeeDee said.

"OK, I just need to get my purse and those books for the pastor. Do you have an umbrella?"

"I'll get it." DeeDee opened the hall closet and took out the big red umbrella. "I'm going to wait in the car," she called to her mother. She paused at the front door and looked out. "It's just barely drizzling," she said to herself. She held the umbrella closed and ran to the car.

It's nice and warm in here, she thought to herself as she slid into the front seat. *I like this new car.* She couldn't help looking at the shiny buttons on the door. *Mother will never know if I play with the buttons or not. She's still in the house.* DeeDee reached over and *click, clack* the locks went down and up. *Click, clack* the locks went down and up again. *Click* went the locks, and then DeeDee heard a noise from the house.

"DeeDee, did you get the umbrella?"

DeeDee quickly climbed out of the car. She pushed the door shut behind her so the seat wouldn't get wet. Then she ran back to the house where her mother was just coming out of the door.

"You did get the umbrella, didn't you, DeeDee?" Mrs. Adams paused before shutting the door.

"Yes, Mother. It's in the car."

Mrs. Adams closed the door behind her. "I didn't want to lock the door until I was sure. Let's go." DeeDee circled around to the other side of the car as her mother reached for the car door handle.

"Hey, why is this locked?" She quickly tried the back door on her side. "DeeDee?"

DeeDee's eyes opened wide. She tried to open the doors on her side, but they were both locked, too. She looked at her mother. "I . . . I was playing with the buttons. I must have locked it accidentally."

Her mother just stared at her. "DeeDee, the keys are in the car. How are we going to get in?"

"Don't you have another key to the car?"

"Yes, I do," her mother sighed. "It's in the house. And the house is locked."

"And your house key is," DeeDee looked down, "in the car."

For a minute, they just stood there and listened to the car's engine running. Then Mrs. Adams sighed again. "We can't get in the car because we can't get in the house. And we can't get in the house because we can't get in the car."

DeeDee almost whispered, "But it was an accident."

"I know you didn't lock the car doors on purpose, DeeDee. But if you had obeyed and not played with the buttons like I asked, the accident wouldn't have happened."

DeeDee eyes filled with tears. "I'm sorry, Mother."

Locked Out!

Mrs. Adams walked around to DeeDee's side of the car. "I'm sorry, too, sweetheart. I forgive you. But we're still going to be late to church, and we have to figure out how to get in the car or the house." She put her arms around DeeDee. "Don't feel too bad. It could be worse."

Just then, it stopped drizzling—and started raining really hard! DeeDee looked up at her mother. "Now, it's worse."

They both laughed and ran to the front porch. "What are we going to do?" DeeDee asked.

"Well, Mrs. Johnson still has a key to our house from the last time she watched it while we were on vacation. If we run to the neighbors and ask to use their phone, we may be able to catch her before she leaves for church."

"We're going to get wet," DeeDee said, looking at the cold rain. Then she took her mother's hand, and they ran next door.

Later, Sabbath School was nearly over when DeeDee opened the door to the Shoebox and came in. Everyone turned and stared. She was quite a sight with her wet hair and dress and muddy shoes. "DeeDee, you're here," Mrs. Shue said politely.

"What happened to you?" Chris called out.

"It's a long story," DeeDee said. She told them about the car and the door locks and disobeying. "And when Mrs. Johnson wasn't home, Mother called the police and asked them to help us. While we were waiting, I walked around the house to see if any of the windows were open or unlocked. But they weren't."

"But how did you get in?" Sammy asked.

"The policeman who came opened the car door with a special tool. Then we hurried here so we wouldn't miss all of Sabbath School."

Mrs. Shue smiled. "Well, you've already learned today's lesson, DeeDee. You learned that when you're sorry for disobeying, you will be forgiven."

DeeDee laughed. "Next week, I want to learn my lesson here in the Shoebox, not out in the rain."

QUESTIONS

1. Does your car have push-button locks?
2. How do you feel when you disobey?
3. Do you ever think it's OK to disobey as long as no one sees you? It's not! God always sees you.
4. Aren't you glad God will always forgive you when you're sorry?

DANIEL WANTS TO EAT RIGHT
Static in the Brain

Daniel and his three friends marched across the desert. They followed the soldiers of Babylon quietly, but they kept looking back toward their home. King Nebuchadnezzar had attacked Judah and captured the city of Jerusalem.

Because the people of Judah kept worshiping idols, God had stopped protecting them. He allowed the army of Babylon to capture Jerusalem and the king. Many of the people were taken away to be slaves, including Daniel and his friends.

When the new slaves arrived in Babylon, King Nebuchadnezzar had a plan. "Bring all the healthy young men from the important families in Jerusalem, including the king's family, to my palace. They will be trained to serve me."

Daniel and his three friends—Hananiah, Mishael, and Azariah—were taken to the palace. They didn't know what would happen to them. But they were treated well. In fact, they were given the best food and drink in the kingdom. "Give all of them food from my own table," the king commanded his chief officer, Ashpenaz. "Teach them to read and write our language."

First Ashpenaz gave them each new names in the language of Babylon. Daniel's new name was Belteshazzar; Hananiah's was Shadrach; Mishael's was Meshach; and Azariah's new name was Abednego. Then they went to eat their first meal.

As soon as the food arrived at their table, Daniel knew there was a problem. "This food isn't right for us," he said. "It's not the food God has told us to eat." He got up to talk to Ashpenaz. "Please allow us to eat the food our God has told us is clean and good. We don't want to eat the meat or rich desserts or to drink the wine. We'll be happy to drink water."

Now God was working on Ashpenaz's heart, and he wanted to be nice to Daniel. But he was afraid of the king. He shook his head. "If you don't eat the king's rich food and drink his wine, you'll become weak. You'll look sick—worse than all the other young men. If the king sees you like that, he will cut off my head."

But Daniel didn't give up. He talked to the guard who watched them. "Please, sir," he said. "Try an experiment with us. Give us only healthy vegetables to eat and water to drink for ten days. Then see if we look better or worse than the other young men."

The guard agreed. So for ten days, Daniel and his friends ate only healthy vegetarian food while the others ate the rich food and meat. They drank the king's good wine while Daniel and his friends drank only water. After ten days, they stood in front of the guard for him to judge.

The guard was shocked! He stared at the four boys. "Look at you!" he said. "Look how healthy and pink your skin is. Look how strong your arms and legs are. Look how your eyes shine. You look much better than these other boys." So he never brought them the king's food again. He brought them only the healthy food and water they asked for.

God blessed Daniel and his friends. They learned many things quickly. They learned more than anyone else. Daniel even learned to understand visions and dreams.

When the three years of their training were finished, Ashpenaz brought all the young men to Nebuchadnezzar. The king looked at each one carefully. He asked many questions. It didn't take him long to see that Daniel, Hananiah, Mishael, and Azariah were smarter than anyone else. He chose them to work for him.

Daniel and his friends handled many important jobs for the king for many years. Nebuchadnezzar told everyone that they were ten times better than any of the wise men or fortune tellers in his kingdom.

Static in the Brain

"Mississippi."

"Jackson," Willie answered quickly.

His dad smiled at him in the rear view mirror. "Right. Do you know all the states and capitals this well? What's the capital of Ohio?"

Willie thought for a minute. "I know this one. It's

Columbus, because when he got to America, he said, 'Oh, hi.' "

Mr. Teller laughed. "That's a good way to remember it." Just then, the car phone buzzed. "Hello," he answered. "Oh, hi, Ted. No, I'm on my way to Willie's school. I'll be back to the office by . . . hello, Ted? Can you hear me?"

Even from where he sat, Willie could hear the crackling from the phone.

"I can't hear you, Ted. I'll try to call you back." Mr. Teller hung up the phone.

"What happened, Dad?"

"There was too much static. I couldn't hear him."

"Is that crackling noise called 'static'?" Willie asked.

"Yes. That crackling noise means that something is interfering with the phone signal. Something is coming between the tower that sends out the phone signal and my antenna. And that keeps the message from getting through. Here, we are. You didn't forget your lunch, did you?"

"No, it's right here in my book bag." Willie wouldn't have forgotten this lunch. Besides his usual desert, he had packed two candy bars. He was going to enjoy lunch today!

Later, Mrs. Thurber said, "Class, we're going to study for our state capitals test with our study partners. Sit close together and talk quietly." Kevin joined Willie at his desk, and they took turns asking and answering questions.

"I'm starving," Kevin said finally. "How long until lunch?"

"Only a few minutes. I'm starving, too. And do I ever have a great lunch." Willie and Kevin were talking about their favorite foods when Mrs. Thurber called for the class's attention.

"Our test will be right after lunch, so don't waste these last few minutes to study. Remember, you'll be asked to match each state with its capital."

"Which state's capital is Frankfort?" Kevin asked.

"Kentucky," Willie answered. "I can remember that because Daniel Boone built a fort in Kentucky. But I think they should have named the capital Danielfort."

At last the lunch bell rang. Willie enjoyed his candy bars so much that he wasn't able to finish his sandwich. "I'm too full," he said to Kevin. "Do you want half?"

"No, I'm full too," Kevin said. "I don't like sandwiches for lunch anyway. But my chips and cookies filled me up."

Mrs. Thurber passed out the test as soon as lunch was over. Willie worked at his paper, trying to remember the names he had repeated over and over. But his eyelids kept drooping and his mind wandered. Before he was finished, the test time was over.

Even before he saw the test grade, Willie knew he had not done well. He showed his father the test on their way home.

"Thirty-one right out of fifty," his dad said at a stop light, as he looked at the test. "It's not too bad, but I thought you knew them better than that. Look, you missed Ohio. You knew that Columbus was the capital of Ohio this morning."

"I know. I just couldn't think very well this afternoon. Well, Mrs. Thurber says we're taking the same test again on Monday. I'll do better next time."

His dad picked up the phone and called home while he drove. "Mom? We're on our way home. Did you need anything at the store?" Willie watched the cars go by as his dad talked. *There must not be any static this time,* he thought.

The next day, in the Shoebox, Mrs. Shue asked a strange question. "What is your favorite food?"

Willie's hand was up first. "Ice cream, especially strawberry."

"Chocolate-chip cookies," Maria said.

Sammy added, "Apple pie."

"German chocolate cake," said Jenny.

"Grasshoppers," Chris shouted.

Everyone stared at Chris. "Grasshoppers?"

"Hey, don't look at me like that," Chris protested. "I mean, Grasshoppers. You know, the mint cookies."

Even Mrs. Shue laughed. "I like mint cookies, too. What if you were having your favorite food for lunch today?"

"Yeaaahh!" everyone cheered.

"And what if you had it again for supper tonight?"

"Yeaaahh!"

"And what if you had it again for breakfast tomorrow?"

"Yuck."

Maria frowned. "I guess even chocolate-chip cookies would stop tasting good if that was all you ever ate."

Mrs. Shue smiled at them all. "What makes desserts and sweets special to us is that we don't have them all the time. Doctors call sweets like cookies and ice cream 'empty' foods because they don't give us what it takes to keep our bodies growing and working right. Now, why does it matter to God that we eat right?"

Static in the Brain

DeeDee raised her hand. "Because God wants us to be healthy and strong so we can be Jesus' hands and do His work."

"That's right. But it's also true that if our body is unhealthy, so is our brain. And since God talks to us through our brain, it's important to keep it working right. Too many sweets interfere with the way our brains work and interfere with God's messages to us."

Wait a minute, thought Willie. "It's like static," he said out loud. "You know, the crackling noise you hear over the radio or phone when something is interfering with the signal. Too many sweets does that to our brains. It makes static, and God's voice can't come through clearly."

"That's very good, Willie. I think you explained it exactly right," Mrs. Shue said.

To himself, Willie kept thinking about static. *That's what happened to me and my test yesterday. Those candy bars and dessert and lunch made so much static in my brain that I couldn't remember the names of the states and capitals I had learned. Well, now I know what to do on Monday.*

Monday, at lunch time, Willie sat across from Kevin and ate his sandwich. Then, he crunched on a carrot.

"Hey, where's your dessert?" Kevin asked.

"I'm skipping my dessert today. It's an experiment to see if I do better on my test."

Kevin stuffed another cookie in his mouth. "What? No way. Dessert doesn't have anything to do with taking tests."

Willie laughed. "Don't be too sure. Let's see if I can get a better grade this time."

DANIEL WANTS TO EAT RIGHT

This time when the tests were handed out, Willie felt wide awake. He zipped right through it. Later that day, he showed his score to Kevin.

"Forty-eight right out of fifty! Do you really think your lunch made a difference?" Kevin asked.

"I'm sure it did," Willie answered.

"Maybe you could teach me about eating the right things," Kevin said with a smile.

"Sure I could. Now, have you ever heard static on the phone or radio . . .?"

QUESTIONS

1. Do you know the capitals of the states? What is the capital of Florida?

2. Do you ever have trouble on tests?

3. Do you ever eat more sweets than you need at lunch?

4. Is the static in your brain keeping you from remembering the answers for your tests? Is it keeping you from hearing God?

CHAPTER

A DREAM AND A STATUE
Terror at the Dentist!

King Nebuchadnezzar woke up unhappy. He stomped around in his bedroom. Then he stomped out to his throne. "Bring me all my wise men, wizards, and fortune tellers," he commanded. Arioch, the captain of his guards, ran to get them.

When the wise men were gathered in front of the throne, Nebuchadnezzar said, "I had a dream. I am very unhappy because I don't know what it means. I want you to tell me."

"Of course we will," his wise men said. "Just tell us your dream, and then we will tell you what it means."

The king shook his head. "No! First, I want you to tell me what I dreamed. Then when you tell me what my dream means, I'll know you are telling the truth. If you can't tell me, I will have you all killed!"

The wise men and wizards looked at each other. They held up their hands. "King, we cannot tell you what you dreamed. No human could do that. Only the gods could tell you, and they don't live on earth to ask."

A DREAM AND A STATUE

Now Nebuchadnezzar got really angry. He turned to Arioch. "Kill them," he said. "Go to the home of each of my wise men and kill them all!"

Arioch took his soldiers and headed to the homes of the wise men. When he got to Daniel's house to kill him, Daniel asked him to explain. When he heard the story, Daniel said, "Please, take me to the king first."

Daniel came to the throne and said, "King Nebuchadnezzar, please give me a little time. Then I will come and tell you your dream and tell you what it means."

The king liked Daniel so he agreed. Daniel went straight home and called his friends together. He explained what had happened. "Now pray with me," he said. "We must ask God to tell us the dream and tell us what it means."

So Daniel, Shadrach, Meshach, and Abednego prayed together. And God told Daniel about the king's dream. Daniel called Arioch. "Don't kill all the wise men. Take me to the king again."

When Daniel was standing in front of the throne again, King Nebuchadnezzar said, "Well? Can you tell me what I dreamed?"

Daniel shook his head. "No," he said. "No person could know this kind of secret. No wise man or wizard or fortune teller. But there is a God in heaven who knows. He has shown you things that will happen in the future. He has told me how to explain your dream."

So Daniel began to tell the king what he had dreamed. "In your dream, you saw a large statue. Its head was made of gold. Its chest and arms were made of silver. The lower body and the top of the legs were made of bronze. The rest of the legs were made of iron. And the feet were made of iron and clay mixed together."

The king clapped his hands. "That's right!" he said.

Daniel went on. "Then you saw a big stone that no one had touched come flying out of the sky. It smashed into the statue's feet, and the whole statue fell apart."

Nebuchadnezzar nodded. "Right," he said. "But what does it mean?"

Daniel spread out his arms. "It tells what will happen in the future," he said. "You are the head of gold. After you, another kingdom will grow strong. But it won't be as great as your kingdom. Then a third kingdom will come after it, and a fourth kingdom after that one. Finally, there will be no more great kingdoms, only small kingdoms that don't mix together."

The king stared with his mouth open. Daniel raised one finger. "But the stone that hit the statue and destroyed it is the God of heaven's kingdom. After all these other kingdoms come and go, God will set up His kingdom. And it will last forever."

King Nebuchadnezzar fell down on his face in front of Daniel. "Your God is the greatest of all gods," he said. "He has told you great secrets." Then he honored Daniel in front of everyone and gave him and his three friends many gifts. And he made Daniel the boss over all the wise men in Babylon.

Because he followed God faithfully and listened to Him, Daniel became one of the most powerful men in the kingdom.

Terror at the Dentist!

"**O***uch!*" Maria's hand went to her jaw.

"What's the matter, Maria?" her mother asked as she flipped the pancakes on the stove.

"Just a little toothache," Maria mumbled. She turned and tried to take another bite of food, but it just hurt too much to chew. She put her fork down.

"I guess I'd better call Dr. Card," Mrs. Vargas said.

Maria's eyes filled with tears. "Oh, Mom, I don't want to go to the dentist. It's starting to feel better already."

Her mother just looked at her. "You know you'll have to go soon. Toothaches don't just go away by themselves."

"I know," Maria agreed, "but I don't want to miss school today. I have a spelling test this morning." She grabbed her books and lunch bag before her mother could change her mind.

When Mrs. Vargas dropped Maria and Chris off at school, she told Maria, "Call me if your tooth keeps bothering you."

Maria tried to ignore the toothache through Bible and Language, but by the end of first recess, it hurt too much. She asked Mrs. Peterson for permission to call her mother. When she got into the car, she said, "I guess I have to go to the dentist now, don't I?"

Mrs. Vargas nodded as she drove. "I called Dr. Card before I left home. One of his patients isn't coming today, so he can see you this morning." She watched the tears form in Maria's eyes again. "Honey, let me tell you exactly what will happen."

"I know what will happen. It will hurt," Maria moaned. "That's what all the kids at school say." Her little sister, Yoyo, reached up and patted her arm.

Mrs. Vargas said, "First you will sit in the dentist's chair, and he'll look at your teeth. Then he may take an X-ray picture of your teeth. But before he can work on fixing the toothache, he has to make the tooth numb."

Maria felt her jaw. "What will that feel like?"

Her mother laughed. "It won't feel at all. You won't feel anything in that part of your mouth. The dentist will make it numb by giving you a shot."

Maria closed her eyes. "That's the part I'm afraid of."

"The shot will hurt a little bit. Dr. Card is very careful and quick, but you may still feel a prick like getting a mean mosquito bite or a splinter. But soon, you won't be able to feel anything on that side of your mouth." Mrs. Vargas continued to drive as she talked, and soon they were parking at the dentist's office. "It will be uncomfortable, even a little painful, but it's the only way to get rid of the toothache."

Before they left the car, she turned and hugged Maria. "I'll be right there with you, Maria. I won't leave you alone." So Maria went into the dentist's office, holding her mother's hand.

The next Sabbath, the Shoebox Kids were studying about the end of time, when Jesus would return. Chris's friend, Ryan, was visiting, and he was confused. "What is the time of trouble?"

Mrs. Shue answered, "The Bible says that near the end of time, just before Jesus returns, the earth will suffer with big problems. There will be famines in some places, where there won't be enough food to eat. There will be diseases and sickness in some places. And there will be many natural disasters, like earthquakes, floods, volcanoes, and fires."

"Wow. That's scary," Ryan said.

Jenny agreed. "It's always seemed scary to me. Whenever I hear adults talking about the end of time, it makes me nervous and afraid."

"I worry about it, too," Willie said. "It always sounds like a lot of people will be starving and hurting."

DeeDee raised her hand. "Are those stories in the Bible supposed to scare us into being good?"

Mrs. Shue looked around at each one. "Jesus isn't trying to scare us into being good. He's just trying to tell us what is going to happen, to warn us ahead of time. It's like . . . it's like . . ."

"I know what it's like," Maria interrupted. "It's like going to the dentist." Everyone turned to look at her. "I had a toothache this week. I didn't want to go to the dentist. I was afraid. I knew that it would hurt."

Sammy agreed. "It always hurts me."

Maria nodded. "Me, too. But my mom reminded me of something I had forgotten. Toothaches don't just go away. The pain may go away for a few hours, but it comes back. You have to go to the dentist to get the cavity fixed."

The kids all nodded.

"The end of time is like that. It has to happen so that Jesus can get rid of sin and sadness forever. It might be painful and make us all unhappy for a while, but it's the only way to get rid of sin."

Chris looked at his sister with a puzzled frown. "But why doesn't Jesus just protect us and keep us happy?"

Terror at the Dentist!

Maria took a deep breath. She wasn't used to explaining all these things. "I guess if Jesus protects everyone like that, He can't get rid of sin. But He does the next best thing for us. When I had to go to the dentist, Mom didn't try to trick me into believing that it wouldn't hurt. She told me exactly what would happen. Then she promised to stay with me until it was over."

"That's what Jesus does," Jenny said. "He tells us what is going to happen at the end of time. It sounds scary, but He promises to stay with us until the end. Right, Mrs. Shue?"

"That's exactly right, Jenny. Maria, you're doing a very good job of explaining this. Did you want to say more?"

"Just this," Maria added. "I didn't want to go to the dentist. But today, I'm very glad I did. I'm glad the toothache is gone for good. And I may not want to think about the end of time, but when Jesus comes, and He gets rid of all the sin and sadness in the world, I'll be very glad the end-of-time problems happened. It will be worth the trouble, even if it is scary and painful."

The Shoebox Kids were all nodding their heads. They understood and agreed. Even Ryan smiled. "That makes sense," he said.

Mrs. Shue had the biggest smile of all. "Thank you, Maria. I couldn't have explained it better. I think you are going to be a teacher for Jesus when you grow up. I know that you have been doing Jesus' work here this morning. It's your turn to cut out a hand print and put it in a glove on our wall."

Maria's Shoebox friends smiled as she cut out her hand print. Chris had the biggest smile of all. He was proud of his sister. "Which glove are you going to put it in?" he asked.

Maria reached up toward a small white glove. "Mom has gloves like this. I want to remember to hold on to Jesus' hand like I held on to her hand when I had to go to the dentist."

"I want to remember that, too," Jenny said.

"And there's one more thing I want to remember," Maria said.

Everyone looked at her again. "What?" they asked.

Maria laughed. "I want to remember to brush my teeth. I learned a lot from the dentist, but I don't ever want to go back."

QUESTIONS

1. Have you ever had a toothache? Were you afraid to go to the dentist?

2. Are you sometimes afraid about the end of time? Does it sound scary?

3. Does it make sense that bad, painful things have to happen to get rid of sin and sadness forever?

4. Did you know that Jesus promises never to leave you when the time of trouble comes?

5. Won't you be glad when Jesus comes?

CHAPTER

THE BURNING FURNACE
Catching Bowling Balls With Your Teeth

As time went by, King Nebuchadnezzar forgot about honoring God. But he didn't forget his dream about the statue. He remembered that Daniel said the head was made of gold. But the rest of the statue wasn't, because Babylon wouldn't last forever.

Nebuchadnezzar didn't like that. He called for his chief builders. "Build me a statue made of gold from top to bottom. I will show everyone that my kingdom will last forever!"

The statue was built on a flat field south of the city. It was about a hundred feet tall and ten feet wide. It was so big that people could see it from miles away. When the statue was completed, Nebuchadnezzar commanded, "All the princes, governors, judges, treasurers, and officials of my kingdom must come to celebrate."

When the special day arrived, all the important people in the whole kingdom came to the big field and stood in front of the statue. The king's announcer spoke up with a loud voice. "When you hear the musical instruments play, you must all bow down and worship the king's golden statue. Whoever doesn't bow down will be thrown into a burning furnace."

When the orchestra began to play, everyone bowed down to worship. Everyone bowed down—except for Shadrach, Meshach, and Abednego. They stood up straight and tall.

Some of the wise men of Babylon were watching the three friends from Judah. They ran to tell the king. "King Nebuchadnezzar, when the music played, we bowed down just like you wanted. But Shadrach, Meshach, and Abednego didn't."

King Nebuchadnezzar was very angry. He called for the three friends to be brought to him. When they were standing in front of him, he said, "Is it true that you did not worship my gold statue? I'm going to give you one more chance. If you don't bow down and worship, I'll throw you into the burning furnace."

But Shadrach, Meshach, and Abednego said, "You're the king. You can throw us into the burning furnace. But the God we serve is strong enough to save us from the fire. And if He does, that will be great. But even if He doesn't, King Nebuchadnezzar, we want you to know that we won't serve your gods. We will not worship your statue of gold."

This made the king even more angry. "Heat up the burning furnace seven times hotter," he commanded. "Then tie up those three men and throw them into the fire."

His strongest soldiers tied Shadrach's, Meshach's, and Abednego's hands together while the fire got hotter. When they pushed the three friends into the furnace, the fire was so hot that it killed the soldiers.

King Nebuchadnezzar watched to see the men go up in smoke. Instead, he saw something he didn't understand. "Didn't we just throw three men into the burning furnace? Why are there four men in there? They're walking around in the flames, not tied up anymore and not being burned up. And the fourth man looks like the Son of God!"

The king called out, "Shadrach! Meshach! Abednego! You servants of the Most High God! Come out of the fire. Come here!"

The three friends walked out of the flames and came right up to the king. He could see that they weren't burned at all. He said, "Praise the God of Shadrach, Meshach, and Abednego! They trusted Him, and He saved them from the fire." Then he commanded that anyone who said anything against their God would be killed.

The three friends from Judah knew they might die if they obeyed God. But they trusted God to help them and take care of them. Because of their faith, the king and many others in Babylon learned about the true God.

Catching Bowling Balls With Your Teeth

"**S**ammy!"

The whisper was so loud that several kids turned and looked at Pete, who was doing the whispering. Finally, Sammy Tan turned and looked at Pete. "You're supposed to be doing your math," he said.

"I am," Pete whispered. "What number are you on?"

"Number eight," Sammy whispered back. "Now, get busy or you're going to have to do it for homework tonight."

Pete grinned. "I'm on number twelve."

Sammy looked at Pete again. He knew that Pete was doing better in math these days, but not that good. "How are you doing them so quickly?" he asked.

Pete slipped his calculator out from under his math book. "This makes it easy," he said.

Sammy frowned. "Mrs. Peterson said not to use our calculators on these problems. She wants us to work them out on paper."

"Well," Pete protested, "it's easier this way. And I want to be finished with all my work before school is over. I don't want to have to do homework this afternoon when you come to my house. Besides, there's nothing wrong with it. Robert and Andy are using their calculators." He slid the calculator back under his book.

Sammy shook his head. "If Robert and Andy were trying to catch bowling balls with their teeth, would you try it too? And if there's nothing wrong with it, why are you hiding your calculator under your book?"

Pete looked down. "I guess you're right, Sammy." He put the calculator in his desk.

Sammy smiled and went back to his math paper. *I guess I did a good thing,* he thought. *I helped Pete decide not to cheat. I guess I was doing Jesus' work this morning.*

Later that afternoon, Sammy and Pete were eating a few chocolate-chip cookies in Pete's backyard when two heads popped up over the back fence. "Hey, Pete, what's going on?" one of the two heads asked.

"Oh, hi, Mike. Hi, Todd. Sammy and I were just trying to decide what to do next. What are you guys doing?"

"We're going hunting with my new BB gun," Todd answered, holding it up over the fence.

"Wow, a BB gun," Sammy said. He ran over to the fence and looked at it more closely.

"What are you hunting around here?" Pete asked.

"Oh, just rats and stuff over in that empty lot by old Mr. McGruder's house," Mike said. "You guys want to come along?"

"I don't know," Pete said. "Mr. McGruder doesn't want kids around."

Sammy looked up from the BB gun. "I want to. Let's go, Pete." So they followed Mike down the street. "Can I try a shot or two?" Sammy asked Todd as they walked.

"Maybe. If we can find something to shoot at," Todd answered. The empty lot was not really empty. It was full of old boards, boxes, and broken bottles. The boys were climbing over a pile when Mike saw something move.

"There's a rat! Shoot him!" he shouted. Todd whirled around to take aim. The rat ran. Todd pulled the trigger. *Snap!* The BB bounced off a tin can. Todd cocked the gun and shot again. *Crack!* The BB broke an old peanut-butter jar.

"You missed him," Pete said as the rat disappeared down a hole.

"But look at this jar," Mike said. "It cracked in half. Let me take a shot at it." Pete and Sammy watched as Mike's shots broke the jar into pieces.

"Let me try it," Sammy asked Todd.

"Wait. Let's set up several bottles on this box and shoot at them," Todd answered. He and Mike began to line up dirty old bottles on the box. Sammy started to help them.

"I'm not so sure this is a good idea," Pete said. "This is not our property. And it might not be safe to shoot at glass like that."

"What wrong with breaking a few bottles?" Mike asked. "Besides, this dump doesn't belong to anyone. Old Mr. McGruder thinks he owns it just because he lives by it."

"Well, the BB could bounce back and hit someone. Or a glass could shatter and cut someone," Pete said. He stood behind the others as Mike and Todd lined up to shoot.

Todd laughed at Pete. "What are you, some kind of chicken? We've done this lots of times." He aimed at the first bottle and fired. *Crack!* The bottle's pieces slid to the ground. Todd handed the gun to Mike.

"Watch me break that big green one," Mike said. *Crack!* Pieces flew into the air. One landed on Sammy's foot.

"Hey, maybe we should back up a little," Sammy said.

Mike laughed. "Are you some kind of chicken, too? A little glass won't hurt you."

Sammy swallowed and said, "When do I get a turn?"

"Just wait," Mike said as he handed the gun back to Todd. They took turns shooting and laughing as Pete and Sammy watched.

Pete grabbed Sammy's arm. "Let's go," he whispered.

"I want to take a shot," Sammy whispered back. Then they heard a shout from across the field and looked up to see a man waving a cane at them.

"It's old Mr. McGruder," Mike said. "Quick, duck down behind these boxes." The four boys ducked and hid. After a minute, Todd began peeking around to see if Mr. McGruder was still there.

"Can we go now?" Pete whispered to Sammy as he tugged on his sleeve. "We're going to get in trouble."

"No, let's wait. There's nothing wrong with shooting a few old bottles. Mike and Todd say it's OK."

Pete looked right at Sammy. "If Mike and Todd said it was OK to catch bowling balls with your teeth, would you try it? Besides, if there's nothing wrong with being here, why are we hiding?"

At first, Sammy just stared at Pete. Then he lowered his eyes and agreed. "Let's get out of here." They stood up and started back across the jumbled boards and boxes. Mr. McGruder was gone. After a minute, they heard a shout from behind them.

"Hey, get back here! McGruder will see you." Sammy glanced back to see Mike and Todd racing off the lot in another direction. Mike turned and yelled, "You two really are chickens."

Sammy turned to his friend. "Thanks, Pete. I've always wanted a BB gun, but my grandmother won't let me have one. I guess I wanted to shoot it so bad that I stopped thinking."

Pete smiled. "Hey, you helped me remember to do the right thing this morning."

"That's right," Sammy agreed. "I was happy to be Jesus' hands this morning and help you. I never thought that Jesus would tell you to help me this afternoon."

Pete just looked at him. "What?"

Sammy laughed. "Let's play catch while I explain." And they did.

QUESTIONS

1. Why did Pete think it was OK to use his calculator? Why did Sammy think it was OK to break bottles in the empty lot?

2. Is it sometimes hard for you to stop and think before you do something that might be wrong?

3. If you aren't sure something is right, do you have to do it just because someone else says it's OK? What if the person who says it's OK is your friend?

4. Did you know that Jesus is always there to help you remember the right thing to do?

CHAPTER

A HAND WRITES ON THE WALL
Mom in Jail!

Belshazzar was the king of Babylon now. He was having a party at the palace for more than a thousand people, and most of them were drunk. The king was drunk too. He decided to do something special for all his guests.

Belshazzar called his servants. "Go and find the gold and silver cups that my grandfather Nebuchadnezzar took from the temple in Jerusalem," he said. "Bring them to me so we can drink our wine from their holy cups. That will prove that our gods are more powerful than their God."

But when they filled those holy cups with wine and lifted them up to drink, something strange happened. A large hand appeared in the air above them! And while they watched, it began to write on the wall in big letters.

The king was so scared that his knees knocked together. His face turned white. He stared at the words on the wall. "Wha . . . wha . . . what does it mean?" he stammered. "What do the words say?"

None of his wise men could read the words, and Belshazzar got even more scared. But his mother came into the room. She said, "Don't be afraid. There is a man in your kingdom who can tell you what this means. He helped Nebuchadnezzar understand dreams. His name is Daniel."

So Belshazzar called for Daniel. "Tell me what these words say and what they mean," he said when Daniel arrived, "and I will give you many gifts."

"King, keep your gifts," Daniel said. "I will tell you what these words mean." Then Daniel reminded him of the stories about Nebuchadnezzar and the messages God had given him. "He learned that the Most High God is the ruler over all countries and kings. You know these stories, King Belshazzar. You know about the God of heaven. But you wouldn't listen to Him. You tried to prove that your gods are stronger than Him."

The king's face got even whiter. He opened his mouth, but no words came out. Daniel kept speaking. "There are four words written on the wall. The first one is *Mene.* It is written twice. It means 'God knows when your kingdom will end.' The third word is *Tekel.* It means, 'You have been judged and found not good enough.' The last word is *Parsin.* It means, 'Your kingdom will be torn in two. It will be given to the Medes and the Persians.' "

Belshazzar knew this wasn't good news. He gave Daniel gifts anyway. But it was too late. Babylon was a big city with two walls around it to protect it from enemy armies. A river flowed right under the wall so that the city always had plenty of water.

Darius, the king of the Medes, had a clever plan. His soldiers dug ditches and turned the water away from the river. Then they went under the city walls where the river used to flow. That same night, Belshazzar, the last king of Babylon, was killed, and the kingdom of Babylon came to an end.

Mom in Jail!

Jenny saw her mother glance in the rear view mirror, but she kept talking. She was explaining why she was late getting ready for school. She wanted to explain, because she knew that she was the reason she was going to be late for class and her mother was going to be late for work.

"So after I found my shoes in the dirty clothes hamper, I ran out on the porch to feed Butterscotch. Then I saw Mr. Garrison in his yard and went to thank him for putting my jacket on the porch after I left it in the yard. Then he asked me if school was . . ."

"Uh, oh," Jenny's mom said. She was still looking in the mirror. Jenny turned and saw a car coming up behind them with flashing red lights on top.

"What's wrong, Mom? Does that police car need to pass us?" Jenny asked as she watched the flashing lights pull up close behind them.

"No," Mrs. Wallace sighed as she signaled to pull over to the side of the road. "I think the officer wants to talk to us." Jenny watched as the police car pulled over behind them. She saw the officer talking into the microphone of her radio.

"Why did she stop us, Mom? Were you driving too fast?"

"I don't know, Jenny. I don't think I was speeding. Let's see what the officer has to say." Most of the officer's brown hair was under her hat as she smiled and asked, "May I see your driver's license, please?"

"Certainly, Officer," Mrs. Wallace said as she reached into her purse. "What seems to be the problem?" she asked.

"Mrs. Wallace, you were driving forty-four miles per hour in a thirty-five-mile-per-hour zone," the officer said.

"Are you sure?" Mrs. Wallace asked. "I don't think I was going that fast. I try to drive carefully on these streets because so many children are walking to school."

"That's what my radar recorded. So I'll be writing you a ticket. Of course, if you wish, you may tell the judge in court how fast you think you were driving. By the way, I am glad to see you both wearing your seat belts."

In a few minutes, they were on their way, but now they were *really* late. Jenny had a hundred questions for her mother. "How fast were you really driving? What did the officer mean about going to court? What happens when you get a ticket?"

"Please, Jenny, stop asking questions. I don't feel like talking about it right now." So Jenny was silent the rest of the way to school.

Jenny had to work hard through the morning to catch up with her class. At lunch, she told her friend Melissa about the ticket. "Mom says she wasn't speeding, but she has to go to court and tell the judge."

Melissa gasped. "The judge! My uncle went to court once, and the judge sent him to jail for two weeks."

"Oh, no! Will the judge send my mom to jail?" Jenny was worried now. One of the other fourth graders, Roger, heard them talking.

Mom in Jail!

"Jenny's mom is going to jail. Jenny's mom is going to jail," he sang out to the rest of the class. He laughed like it was the funniest joke in the world. But Jenny didn't laugh. She put her head down and tried not to cry.

"Hush, Roger," Melissa said. "Judges put only bad people in jail, and Jenny's mother is a good person." She patted Jenny's arm. "Don't let him upset you. I'm sure the judge will be nice to your mother."

Jenny was still a little upset about it after school, but she was almost too busy to worry. She took Butterscotch out to play for a few minutes and picked up Mr. Garrison's newspaper like she did almost every day after school. She put it next to his front door and went on with her chores.

She remembered to be worried later that night, so she crawled onto the couch next to her mom. "Mom, when do you have to go and talk to the judge?"

Her mom slid back so that Jenny could snuggle in close. "I go to traffic court a week from next Thursday. It's after school, so you could go with me if you want to."

"Oh, no," Jenny shivered. "I'd be afraid to. I'm afraid the judge might put me in jail."

Her mom looked puzzled. "Why would you think that?"

"Because if you were driving too fast, it's my fault. I made us late because I wasn't ready to go."

"Jenny! It's not your fault. No matter why we were late, I was driving, and I'm responsible for how fast I was going. The speeding ticket is certainly not your fault."

Jenny felt better, but she was still worried. "What will the judge do to you?" she asked quietly.

Mrs. Wallace brushed back Jenny's blonde hair with her fingers as she explained. "The judge will listen to the police officer and to me, and then decide if I was speeding. If he thinks I was, I will have to pay a fine."

"And that's all? He won't put you in jail or anything?"

"Judges do put people in jail, Jenny, but only when they hurt or steal from others."

Jenny felt much better now. "Then you aren't worried at all?"

"Well, I don't want to pay a fine," her mother admitted. "We need the money I make for food and things. So I hope the judge agrees with me. But if not, I'll still pay without arguing. I know the police officers and judges are just trying to keep us safe from dangerous drivers."

"I'll hope the judge agrees with you, too," Jenny said.

That day at the courthouse, Jenny was worried again. She saw police officers with guns leading people away to jail in handcuffs. She held her mother's hand tightly as they walked into the courtroom and sat down.

Just then, a man in a uniform stood up at the front and said, "All rise. Traffic court is now in session, the Honorable Judge William Garrison presiding."

Jenny watched, and her mouth fell open. There was Mr. Garrison, her neighbor, dressed in a black robe. "Look, Mom! There's Mr. Garrison! What's he doing here?"

"Why, I guess he's the judge. I didn't know he was a judge in this court," Mom said with a smile.

Jenny just sat back and grinned. She wasn't worried any more.

On the way home, Mrs. Wallace said, "You know, Jenny, a lot of people, even grown-ups, worry about the judgment in heaven when God will decide who will live with Him forever."

"That is kind of scary," Jenny admitted. "Because I know I have done the wrong things sometimes."

"It can be scary, until you remember who is going to do the judging. Jesus is our Judge! And since He loved us so much that He died for us, you know He wants us in heaven."

Jenny smiled. "I wasn't worried anymore when I saw that my friend Mr. Garrison was your judge. I can trust him to be fair and kind. And I know I won't be afraid when my Friend Jesus judges me."

"I won't either," her mother said. "Now, let's stop and have pizza for supper."

"OK," Jenny agreed, with a glance at the cars behind them, "but let's drive nice and slow."

QUESTIONS

1. Do you ever make your family late because you aren't ready? Think about how you can plan ahead.

2. Have you ever been in the car when the driver got a ticket? Was it scary?

3. Would you be afraid of a judge? What if the judge was your friend?

4. Did you know that your friend Jesus will be your judge at the end of time?

CHAPTER

DANIEL AND THE LIONS' DEN
Danger in the Water

When King Darius took over the kingdom of Babylon, he needed help to run the whole country. He chose 120 governors to be in charge, but he chose three men to supervise his governors. He chose Daniel to be one of those supervisors.

Daniel still faithfully worshiped God. Three times each day, he opened his windows and prayed to God. God blessed Daniel and everything he did. So Daniel was a very wise man. He was honest, and he worked hard. Before long, the king planned to put him in charge of the whole kingdom.

Some of the other officials were jealous of how much the king liked Daniel. They didn't want Daniel to be in charge of them. "Let's find out something bad about Daniel and tell the king," they said to each other. "Then the king will change his mind." So they watched everything Daniel did.

But Daniel was honest and kind. He didn't do anything wrong.

So the jealous officials came up with another plan.

DANIEL AND THE LIONS' DEN

"The only strange thing Daniel does is pray to his God. Let's set up a trap for him." They went to King Darius and said, "O Mighty King, all of your officials owe loyalty to you. You are more powerful than any god, so let's make a law that no one in the whole kingdom can pray to anyone but you for thirty days. If anyone breaks this law, they will be thrown into the lions' den."

This made Darius feel very good and very proud. He signed the new law happily and sent his officials to announce it everywhere.

Daniel heard about Darius's new law. He knew about the lions. But he did the same thing he did every day. He went to his room and opened his windows. Then he knelt down and prayed just like he always did.

The jealous officials were waiting and watching. As soon as they saw Daniel kneel by his window, they ran to the king. "King, your new law says that no one may pray to anyone but you for thirty days. But Daniel is praying to his God. Your new law says that he must be thrown into the lions' den."

The king's mouth fell open. Now he understood why those officials wanted him to make the new law! It made him very unhappy, because he liked Daniel. He tried to think of a way around the law. But the laws of his kingdom could not be broken, not even by the king.

Finally, sadly, he gave his guards the order to arrest Daniel. He met them at the entrance to the lions' den. "I'm sorry, Daniel," King Darius said. "I hope the God you serve so faithfully is able to protect you from these lions." Then the guards lowered Daniel down into the lions' den. A large stone was rolled up and put in place over the opening so that there was no way out.

The king went back to his palace. His supper was served, but he didn't eat any. He wasn't hungry. He wasn't sleepy either. Darius stayed awake all night. As soon as it was light, he ran back to the lions' den.

"Move that stone!" he commanded his guards. When they rolled it away, he stared down into the dark. "Daniel, servant of the living God," he called, "was your God able to save you from the lions?"

Daniel's voice came up loud and strong. "O King, live forever! My God sent His angels to keep the lions' mouths closed. They didn't hurt me, because God knows that I didn't do anything wrong."

The king started smiling. "Pull him up out of there," he commanded the guards. When Daniel stood beside him, it was easy to see that he wasn't hurt at all. The king gave the guards another command. "Find those jealous officers. Bring them here and throw them into the lions' den." This time the lions' mouths weren't closed. The officers were quickly killed.

Then King Darius made a new law. He had it read to all the people of his kingdom. "Everyone must respect Daniel's God because He is the living God. He saved Daniel from the lions."

Danger in the Water

"**Y**ahoo!" Chris yelled as he swung out over the dark blue water of the lake. When he let go of the rope, he dropped in with a big splash.

"Is it cold?" his sister Maria asked when he popped up. She and little Yoyo stood on the dock and watched Chris swim toward them.

"It's perfect," Chris answered as he grabbed the rope and waded back to the dock ladder. "I'm doing it again." He loved their trips to Hobart Lake. And what he loved most was this rope swing. There was nothing like soaring through the air and then splashing down into the water. He wrapped his hands around the big knot, jumped up, and flew out over the water again.

"Mama, can I swing too?" Yoyo called out. Mr. and Mrs. Vargas were getting settled in their lawn chairs near the lake shore.

"Yes, Yoyo," her mother answered. "But since you can't swim, you must keep your life jacket on any time you are down here by the water. Maria, will you wait out in the water after your jump and help Yoyo?"

"Sure, Mom. Come on, Yoyo, you're after me." Then, Maria swung out over the water and splashed in. On the dock, Chris helped Yoyo get the rope and showed her how to hang on. Maria waited and said, "When I say 'Now!' then you let go. OK?"

Yoyo nodded and grabbed the rope. Then she jumped. *Wheee, this is fun,* she thought, as she flew through the air. She almost forgot to let go when she heard Maria shout, "Now!" She looked down and saw Maria a long way below her. Then she closed her eyes and turned loose of the rope.

Splash! Yoyo hit the water and almost disappeared behind the wave. She didn't really go under water because her life jacket held her up. Maria was right there to grab her.

Danger in the Water

"Did you like it? Do you want to do it again?" Maria asked, as she brushed the water off Yoyo's face.

"Yes, yes, yes!" Yoyo shouted. The three of them took turns as their mom and dad talked and rested in their lounges. After a while, Mrs. Vargas said, "Kids, we're going in to fix lunch now. Maria and Chris, keep an eye on Yoyo." Then they walked up to the cabin.

Chris and Maria swam around a little longer and caught Yoyo when she wanted to swing on the rope. "I'm getting cold," Maria said suddenly. "I'm going to sit in the sun for a while."

"Wait for me," Chris replied. "Let's go sit in Mom's and Dad's chairs. Yoyo, are you coming with us?"

Yoyo was glad they were getting out since she needed to run up to the bathroom in the cabin. "I'll be back in a minute," she called, as she scurried away, water still dripping off her life jacket.

Chris and Maria settled back in the sunshine and relaxed. "This is great," Chris said. "No spelling, no math, no language, and best of all, no homework."

"Right," Maria agreed, with her towel wrapped around her and her eyes closed. "And there's only a few days of school left. Soon we'll be doing nothing like this every day."

While the two of them lay there, dreaming about the summer, Yoyo came back out of the cabin and walked quietly down to the dock. Her mom had helped her put her life jacket back on after her stop at the bathroom. But as she walked out to the edge of the dock, Yoyo wondered what it would be like to go under the water. She knew how to hold her breath. And she was tired of just bobbing on the surface with her life jacket. Since Yoyo was not the kind of girl to worry or be afraid, she just slipped off her life jacket and jumped in.

"Hey, who jumped in the water?" Chris asked as both he and Maria sat up and looked around. They didn't see anyone. "Aren't Mom and Dad still in the cabin?"

"And Yoyo's still there too, isn't she?" Maria asked. "Besides, if she jumped in, we could see her and her life jacket on top of the water."

Suddenly Chris froze. When Maria looked at him, he pointed. "Isn't that her life jacket there on the dock?"

For a second, they just stared. Then both jumped up at the same time. "Dad, Mom, come quick!" Maria was shouting as she ran toward the cabin. At the same time, Chris was running toward the dock.

Yoyo was floating near the bottom of the lake, not far from the dock. It wasn't really very deep there, and she still wasn't afraid. In fact, she thought the bottom of the lake was pretty. She even saw a fish swim by! But very soon, she began to wonder how Chris and Maria got back to the surface when they wanted to breathe.

Chris ran out to the edge of the dock and stared down, trying to see where Yoyo might be. But he wasn't just staring. He was praying. "Oh, Jesus, help me find Yoyo. Don't let her drown. Help me find her." He was still praying as he jumped out into the water.

By now, Maria and her parents were racing down from the cabin, shouting for Yoyo and Chris. Yoyo was still near the bottom, trying to flap her arms like she had seen Chris do when he was swimming underwater. Now, she was starting to get a little worried.

Danger in the Water

Chris, who was *very* worried, swam out from the dock, peering down into the dark water. With one last prayer, he took a deep breath and dove down. The first thing his fingers touched was Yoyo's arm. It took him only a second to grab her. Then he kicked for the surface.

As soon as Chris's head popped up out of the water, his father was there, grabbing him and Yoyo. Then in one big swimming bear hug, they made their way back to the shore. There, Maria and her mother were laughing and crying at the same time.

"Yoyo, are you OK?" Mrs. Vargas grabbed her and hugged her tight. Yoyo laughed with everyone else and said, "Daddy, why did you go swimming with all your clothes on?"

They all laughed. "You silly girl, I was going in to find you, but Chris already did. You did great, son. You did exactly the right thing. I'm very proud of you." He reached out and hugged Chris again.

Chris's mother turned to hug him, too. "Thank God you were there, Chris. I know God used you for an angel today. I love you very much. And you, Maria, you did the right thing, too. Both of you make me very proud."

Finally, the excitement wore down, and they walked toward the cabin and their lunch. Mrs. Vargas explained to Yoyo over and over how important it was to wear her life jacket. Chris and Maria told about hearing the splash and seeing Yoyo's life jacket. Yoyo even told them about the fish she saw. Chris shared with them how he had prayed. "I guess the angels were with me, because when I dove in, I couldn't see anything. But I swam right to where Yoyo was."

When he asked for God's blessing on the food, Mr. Vargas thanked God for watching over Yoyo and for helping Chris find her.

"Hey," Maria said to Chris, "Now you'll have something to tell them at the Shoebox this Sabbath. You really were Jesus' hands today. He used your hands to find Yoyo and save her."

Chris laughed. "I'm just glad that Jesus' angels know how to swim underwater."

QUESTIONS

1. Do you know how to swim? Be sure to wear your life jacket until you're a good swimmer.

2. One of the most important rules about swimming is to never swim alone. You never know when you might need help!

3. Did you know that Jesus' angels are waiting to protect you from danger?

4. Can you think of a time when angels helped you or protected you? If you can't, ask your mom or dad if they can.

CHAPTER

A SPECIAL QUEEN FOR A SPECIAL TIME, PART ONE

DeeDee and Queen Esther

The Jews had been taken away from their land of Judah long years before. Because they would not obey God, He let them be captured. Now after seventy years, God wanted them to move home. He caused King Cyrus of Persia to write a law that let all the Jews move back to Judah.

But not all the Jews wanted to move back. Many of them had nice homes and businesses in Persia and in other countries. So they stayed where they were. And even though God wanted them to move, He still protected those who worshiped Him.

Now King Xerxes was the ruler of Persia. A Jewish girl named Esther lived near his palace in the city of Susa. Esther's parents were dead, but she still had a home. Her older cousin Mordecai adopted her and raised her as his daughter.

King Xerxes was very rich, and he had a beautiful queen. But she made him very angry so he threw her out of the palace. Then he announced a contest. "I am looking for a new queen. Bring all the most beautiful young women in my kingdom to my palace. After I see each one, I will choose one to be my new queen."

Young women from all over the kingdom were brought to the palace in Susa. But one girl didn't have to go very far—Esther was so beautiful that she was taken to the palace also!

Before she left, Mordecai talked to her. "I'll come near the palace and watch for you, Esther," he said. "But don't tell anyone that you are a Jew."

So Esther said nothing. She went to the palace and learned everything about being a queen. And after he had seen all the young women, the king chose Esther to be his new queen!

Mordecai worked at the palace gate so he got to see Esther sometimes. One day while he was working, he heard two men planning to kill the king! He told Esther, and she told the king. The two men were arrested, and the king was safe. The whole story was written down in the king's daily record books.

About the same time, King Xerxes chose a man named Haman to be his highest official. Haman was so important that he wanted everyone to bow down whenever he went by. And everyone did—everyone except Mordecai. Mordecai refused to bow down to anyone except God.

Every time Haman went by the palace gates, everyone bowed down except Mordecai. That made Haman very angry. When he heard that Mordecai was a Jew, he said to himself, "I'll get rid of all the Jews—including Mordecai." So Haman visited the king.

"King Xerxes," Haman said, "there are some people in your kingdom who don't obey your laws. They insist on being different from anyone else. They keep their own ways and their own customs. They are the Jews, and if we get rid of them, your kingdom will be a better place."

Then Haman asked the king to make a new law that all the Jews in the kingdom would be killed on the same day. The king didn't know that Queen Esther and Mordecai were Jews. He gave Haman the special ring he used when he made new laws. "Do whatever you want," the king said.

So Haman made the new law. He sent letters to all the lands of the kingdom saying that the Jews should be killed on a certain day. When they heard about the law, the Jews everywhere cried out and prayed to God for help.

Could anyone help the Jews escape Haman's terrible plans?

DeeDee and Queen Esther

"**W**hat are you going to be when you grow up?" Mrs. Shue asked the question, and almost everyone had an answer.

Sammy said, "I plan to be a scientist or a math teacher."

Jenny said, "I want to be either a secretary or a doctor."

"I don't know if I want to be an animal doctor or a people doctor," Willie said.

Chris said, "I can't decide if I want to be the President of the United States or a garbage collector." Everyone laughed.

Maria was sure about her plans. "I'm going to own a roller skating rink so I can skate whenever I want."

A SPECIAL QUEEN FOR A SPECIAL TIME

Mrs. Shue listened. "I wonder if anyone ever asked Esther what she was going to be when she grew up. Chris was kind of joking about being the president, but I wonder if Esther ever thought about being the queen."

DeeDee listened to the others, but she didn't say anything. She was busy thinking to herself. *I wish I knew what to be when I grow up. I wonder how someone knows what God wants? What if God wants me to be a doctor and I want to be a singer or an ice skater? I wish I could talk to Esther,* she thought. *I'd ask her.*

* * * * *

DeeDee's mind wandered as she thought about sitting in a huge stone palace with Queen Esther, the girl who followed God's plan for her life and saved her people.

"Esther, how did you know God's plan for your life? Did you know He wanted you to be a queen?"

Esther turned from the flowers she was arranging in a solid gold vase. "DeeDee, when I was your age, I had no idea what God wanted for my life. In fact, for a while I thought I hated God. My parents were killed when I was very young. Remember, it was my uncle Mordecai who raised me."

"I forgot about that," DeeDee said sadly.

Esther picked up the vase and placed it on the stone window sill. "I didn't think God cared about me at all. But Uncle Mordecai kept telling me that I was a special person and that God had a special plan for me. I learned again that God really did love me, and I began to wonder what He wanted me to be when I grew up."

DeeDee nodded. "I wonder that, too."

DeeDee and Queen Esther

"Uncle Mordecai taught me something important. He said that I should just worry about doing my best at my work each day and let God worry about the future." Esther motioned for a servant to bring her more flowers. "So I did. At first, I was sure that God planned for me to spend my whole life taking care of my uncle's house."

"How did you become the queen?"

Esther smiled at the memory. "When Uncle Mordecai told me that the king was choosing a new queen and that I should enter the contest, I laughed. I knew that there was no way the king would choose me. But I went anyway to make my uncle happy."

DeeDee watched Esther with dreamy eyes. "Yet the king chose you to be the queen. It must have been love at first sight."

Queen Esther laughed. "I guess so. I had never even imagined being a queen. Every day I thanked God for blessing me with all this," she added with a wave of her hand, "I wondered why He gave it to me."

"It must have been wonderful," DeeDee said. "But then Haman almost ruined everything."

"Oh, yes. When Haman started his plan to kill all the Jewish people, he didn't know I was one of them. I didn't know what to do. Then Uncle Mordecai made me think. Maybe God had made me the queen just because this was going to happen. Maybe His plan for my life was to help Him save my people."

"Weren't you afraid?"

Esther had to sit down beside DeeDee. "I was scared to death! You know, when I went in speak to the king, he could have ordered his guards to kill me if he didn't want to see me. But do you know why I went in to the king's throne anyway?"

DeeDee shivered and shook her head silently.

"Since I believed that God had a plan for my life, I knew that I had to try to follow it. I believed that God wanted me to take care of my uncle's house, so I worked hard and did my best. I believed that God wanted me to be queen, so I tried to be the best queen I could be."

"I see," DeeDee said. "Since you wanted to follow God's plan for your life, you tried to do your best at whatever you were doing."

"That's right," Esther said. "And since I had always been trying to follow God's plan, it seemed right to keep following it and go see the king to try to save my people. It was scary, but I did it anyway. I decided to trust God's plan."

DeeDee nodded, but she was still a little confused. "But how could you be sure what God's plan for you was?"

Queen Esther had to think about that. She motioned to a servant who brought them sparkling apple juice in silver goblets. "The same way you are sure about God's plan for you, DeeDee. You read your Bible and pray to stay in touch with your Friend, God, everyday. You listen to your family and friends who care about you, like I listened to Uncle Mordecai. And you listen to your own heart, where God speaks to you. He gave you talents and dreams."

"I guess you're right. God gave me the talents of playing the piano and singing. But sometimes I dream about being a doctor or a scientist. Oh, I don't know which to do."

DeeDee and Queen Esther

Esther laughed and patted DeeDee's arm. "But don't you see? You don't have to know all that today. All you have to do today is the best you can at home and at school. Let God worry about the future. When the time is right, He'll let you know what to do. I'm very happy I followed His plan for me. I know it will make you happy, too."

* * * * *

"DeeDee. DeeDee, are you with us?" Mrs. Shue was calling as DeeDee blinked and looked up. For a second, she was surprised to see all her friends around her in the Shoebox instead of the stone walls of Queen Esther's palace. Then she looked around and smiled.

Mrs. Shue went on. "I was asking what you think God's plan for your life might be."

"Oh, I know that already," DeeDee answered.

Everyone was surprised to hear that. "Oh, really," Mrs. Shue said. "What is it?"

DeeDee smiled like a queen. "Right now, His plan is for me to work and study and do my best. That way I'll be ready for whatever He has planned for me next."

QUESTIONS
1. What are you going to be when you grow up?
2. Did you know that God has a plan for your life?
3. How did Esther know what God wanted her to do?
4. How can you follow God's plan for your life today?

CHAPTER

A SPECIAL QUEEN FOR A SPECIAL TIME, PART TWO
Tornado Warning!

When Mordecai heard about the law, he contacted Queen Esther. "You must talk to the king for us," he said. "You must tell him to save our people."

Esther shook her head. "I'm afraid," she said. "You know the law. If anyone goes in to see the king without being invited, they can be killed—even me. I would be allowed to live only if the king holds out his golden scepter to me."

Mordecai said, "We are all in danger of being killed. And it might be that you were chosen queen just so you could help your people at this time."

So Esther agreed. "Ask every Jew in the city to pray with me for three days. Then I will go to the king." After three days, Esther dressed up in her nicest dress and walked to the king's throne room. She stood there waiting and praying—she was still scared.

But when the king saw her, he smiled and held out his golden scepter. "What can I do for you?" he asked. "I'll give you anything you want."

Esther smiled too. "I just want you to come to a dinner party tonight. I want you and Haman to be my guests."

So the king and Haman went to Esther's party that night. It was very nice. "Now," the king said to Esther, "tell me what you really want."

Esther smiled again. "Come to another dinner party tomorrow night, and I'll tell you." So the king and Haman agreed to come back the next night.

Haman felt very important that night. But on his way home, he passed Mordecai. Of course, Mordecai didn't bow down. Suddenly, Haman was angry again. He told his friends and family about what happened. "Build a big platform to hang someone," they said. "Then tomorrow, ask the king to let you hang Mordecai." Haman liked the idea so much that he hired builders to begin right away.

At the same time, the king was having trouble falling asleep. He called for someone to read to him. "Read from my palace record books," he said. And he heard the story of how Mordecai had reported that two men were planning to kill the king. "How was Mordecai rewarded for what he did?" the king asked.

"He wasn't rewarded at all," the reader reported. The king decided to reward Mordecai right away.

The next day, Haman came in to ask the king if he could hang Mordecai. But before he could ask, the king asked him a question. "What should I do for someone I really want to honor?" he asked Haman.

Oh, Haman thought, *the king is talking about me!* "Well," he answered, "I'd put the king's robe on this person, put him on the king's horse, and have a servant walk him through the city telling everyone how important he is."

"That's a great idea," the king said. "I want you to do exactly that to Mordecai, the man who works at the palace gate."

So Haman had to walk around the city leading the king's horse with Morecai on it and telling everyone how important Mordecai was. When he got home, he was very unhappy. But, at least, he got to go to Queen Esther's dinner party.

At the party, King Xerxes asked again, "What can I give you, Esther?"

Queen Esther took a deep breath. "Give me my life and the lives of my people. Someone wants to kill us all."

The king jumped up. "Who wants to kill you?" he demanded.

Esther pointed straight at Haman. "He is our enemy. Haman is planning to have all the Jews killed."

The king was so angry that he had Haman hung on the big platform Haman had built at his own house. Then he gave Mordecai Haman's job. Even the king couldn't change the law that let people kill Jews. But he told Mordecai to send out letters to tell the Jews to defend themselves against anyone who attacked them.

God chose Esther to be queen so that He could protect His people in their time of trouble.

Tornado Warning!

Crack! Crash! Jenny ducked and closed her eyes as the lightning struck close outside. "Mom, did you see that? Mom, where are you?" Jenny ran down the hall. She found her mother bent over the radio in the kitchen.

"Shhh," Mrs. Wallace hissed. They listened closely to the crackling sound of a man's voice.

"Once again, a tornado watch has been issued for our area. A tornado watch means that these thunderstorms could produce tornadoes, so to be safe, stay indoors away from windows, and keep listening for more information."

Jenny looked at her mom. "Is a tornado coming here?" she asked.

Her mom turned and hugged her tight. "No. Not yet anyway."

In her home outside of town, Mrs. Shue was worried, too. She stopped washing her dishes for a moment and prayed. "Father in heaven, please watch over Your people in our town today and protect them from this storm. And please, send extra angels to watch over our Shoebox Kids."

Over in his front yard, Chris was playing catch with his friend Ryan. They had heard the rumble of thunder, but it still seemed far away. "All right, Chris. Get ready for a fastball," Ryan shouted. "Chris?"

Chris was staring up at the sky. "Ryan, have you ever seen the sky look green like that?" Ryan stared up, too.

"That is weird," Ryan agreed. The sky seemed to get darker every second. Then a lightning bolt ripped across the dark green clouds. Thunder crashed, and both boys made the same decision.

"I'd better go home. See you later."

Willie and his dad were at home watching television when their program was interrupted. "A tornado warning has just been issued for Mill Valley. A tornado has been spotted moving toward the town. People living there should take cover immediately. I repeat; a tornado has been seen near Mill Valley."

Willie's eyes opened wide. He looked at his dad. "Is that here?"

"That's here," He explained again as Willie's mom rushed into the room. "Let's go down to the end of the hall, just like we practiced." Coco joined the family as they sped down to the end of the hall and waited. And prayed.

Jenny and her mom heard the warning on their radio. "Where do we go?" Jenny cried.

"To my bathroom," her mom answered as she grabbed Jenny's arm and they ran down the hall. Mrs. Wallace dashed into Jenny's room and yanked the mattress off her bed. "We'll get in the tub and put this mattress over our heads," she explained to Jenny as they dragged it toward the bathroom.

"Mom, I'm afraid," Jenny cried as she wriggled down into the tub.

"Me, too, Jenny," her mom said quietly. "Let's pray and ask Jesus to be with us." She wrapped her arms around Jenny and prayed: "Dear Jesus, please be with us and keep us safe. Be with all your people in this dangerous time."

At Sammy Tan's house, they had heard the radio warning and headed down the stairs to their basement. Luckily, DeeDee's family was out of town.

When Chris ran into his house, Maria was looking out the front windows. "This is scary," she said. "Mom and Yoyo went down to the store just a few minutes ago. Dad isn't home yet."

"Maybe we should listen for a weather report on TV," Chris said. He reached past the vase of roses on the phone table and picked up the remote control. With a push of a button, the TV snapped on.

The news person was speaking. "This just in. At least two tornadoes have been spotted in the Mill Valley area. If you live in that area, seek shelter immediately."

Chris and Maria stared at each other. "Where do we go?" Maria whispered. The man on the TV kept talking.

"If you are outdoors, get inside if you can. If not, lie down in the nearest ditch and cover your head. If you are inside, move away from all windows and glass. Take shelter in the basement if you have one, or in a bathroom, hall-way, or closet that is small and well-protected. I repeat . . ." Suddenly, the TV and all the lights went out.

Maria screamed and ran toward Chris. The wind howled outside. Then Maria remembered. "The closet under the stairs! Mom said we should hide there if a tornado was coming." They ran toward the stairs, but the front door flew open and banged into the wall. Maria screamed again.

"It's Mom!" Chris shouted. She ran in, holding Yoyo, and Chris helped her push the door shut. "The news says to watch out for tornadoes," Maria said.

"I know," she started to answer, but suddenly the wind stopped blowing, and everything was very still. Chris turned and looked out the window.

"Mom, it's a tornado!" He could see the tornado's long funnel reaching down toward the ground like an elephant's trunk. As he watched, the tornado moved closer. It was coming straight toward them!

"Run!" Mrs. Vargas shouted. Still carrying Yoyo, she pushed Chris and Maria ahead of her. "Run to the stairs closet!"

Tornado Warning!

They ran and dove on the closet floor. Mrs. Vargas threw her arms around everyone and tried to cover them. Yoyo was crying. Chris and Maria were too scared to cry. Their mom prayed out loud. "God, send Your angels to protect us. Protect all Your people from this terrible storm."

Then they heard a loud noise. It sounded like a train was coming right through their house. After a minute, the roaring wind died away, and everything was quiet. "Are you Ok?" Mrs. Vargas asked each one. Everyone was, so she turned the doorknob and opened the door just enough to peek out. "Oh, no," she whispered. Then she just stared. Finally, Yoyo leaned past her and pushed the door the rest of the way open.

"Mama, why is the sky in our living room?" Yoyo asked, looking up. "Where did the ceiling go?"

Chris and Maria pushed their way out of the closet. "Mom! The roof is gone!" Maria shouted. Chris stared at the couch and chair that were still sitting in place. The phone still sat on its table beside the couch, but all the petals from the roses were gone. Suddenly, the phone rang.

At almost the same time, someone starting pounding on the front door. "Is anyone hurt? Are you OK?" a voice shouted.

Chris reached the door just as it opened. Ryan and his mother were coming in. "Is everyone OK?" Ryan's mother asked. Meanwhile, Yoyo ran to answer the phone.

"Hello? Oh, hi Daddy. Daddy, we had a torpedo. And now the sky is in the living room." She listened for a second and called her mother. "Dad wants to talk to you, Mom."

Ryan was amazed. "Chris, where did you guys hide? This is weird." As Chris told him all about it, a light rain started. His mom got off the phone and herded everyone out the door.

"Dad says to go to the neighbors and wait for him." She looked at Ryan's mom.

"Of course. Come to my house. Quick before we're soaked."

Later, after Mr. Vargas got home, they were settling down in the guest room at Ryan's house when Mrs. Shue drove over to check on them.

After hugging her Shoebox Kids, she said, "I've got good news and bad news. The good news is, I've heard from all the other Shoebox Kids and everyone is OK. Only your house was damaged. But we can be thankful that God watched over us all and protected us."

"Amen," Mrs. Vargas agreed. "We could have been killed."

Mrs. Shue went on. "The bad news is, the church was damaged. I understand that the main church looks worse than your house."

"Oh, no," Maria gasped. "What about the Shoebox? Is it still there?"

"I don't know," Mrs. Shue said. "Tomorrow we'll have to go see."

(To be continued.)

QUESTIONS

1. Do you know what to do if there is a tornado warning in your town?

2. Does your family have a plan in case of a tornado? If not, help your parent make a good, safe, plan.

3. God watches over His people during times of trouble. Isn't it nice to be in God's family?

4. God is especially close to us when something bad happens. Aren't you glad He loves you that much?

CHAPTER

NEHEMIAH BUILDS THE WALLS
Fighting to Help

When King Cyrus of Persia allowed the Jews to return to Jerusalem, many of them stayed in Persia. Only 42,000 Jews returned. For years, those who went back to Judah had problems with the people who lived nearby, but finally they finished building the new temple in Jerusalem. Now the Jews had their city back with its strong walls and a new temple.

After the time of Esther, many more Jews returned to Judah. They were led by Ezra, a priest who wanted the people to learn about God and His laws again. But a war started between the Persians and the people who lived near Jerusalem. During the fighting, much of the wall around Jerusalem was torn down. The wooden gates to the city were burned. No one could feel safe inside.

Nehemiah was a Jew who worked in the king's palace in Persia. It was his job to serve the king's drinks and to make the king laugh. But when he heard about the fighting in Jerusalem, Nehemiah was very sad. He was so sad that the king asked, "What's wrong, Nehemiah? Something seems to be bothering you."

NEHEMIAH BUILDS THE WALLS

Nehemiah didn't want to get in trouble. But he just couldn't pretend to be happy for the king. "How can I be happy?" he said. "My home city is ruined. The walls have been knocked down, and the gates were burned."

The king looked at Nehemiah. "What would you like to do about it?" he asked.

Nehemiah didn't have to think very long. "If it's OK with you, King, I'd like to go and help build the walls again."

It was OK with the king. He even sent along all the supplies Nehemiah would need to do the repairs!

When Nehemiah arrived, he found that some of the people living near Jerusalem didn't want the walls repaired. They didn't want the Jews to have a strong, safe city again. The leaders of these people were Sanballat, Tobiah, and Geshem.

But Nehemiah did have help. The Jews living in Jerusalem wanted their walls fixed. Nehemiah gave each family a part of the wall to repair. They all worked together and worked hard. Soon the wall was halfway up.

Then Sanballat brought an army to fight the wall builders. So Nehemiah said, "We must work together in pairs. One person must be ready to fight while the other person keeps on building." Nehemiah had people with trumpets watching at different places along the wall. If they saw any enemy soldiers, they blew the trumpets, and everyone came together to fight. The people wore their armor all day, even while they worked. When they slept, they wore just their clothes and kept their weapons by their sides.

Since he couldn't stop the Jews by fighting, Sanballat tried something else. "Nehemiah, people are saying that you want to build a strong city so you can be king," Sanballat said. "Let's get together and talk about that."

But Nehemiah knew what Sanballat was doing. "You're just making things up," he said. "I have an important job to do. Why should the work stop while I talk to you?"

Other people tried to stop Nehemiah also, but he would not turn away from his work. He kept everyone working together. In just fifty-two days, the walls were finished.

Nehemiah called all the people together by the main gate of the city. Ezra read to them from the Book of the Law of Moses. "We promise to love and obey God," the people shouted.

No one believed that the walls could be fixed that quickly. Even Nehemiah's enemies thought it was a miracle. "Surely this work was done by God," they said.

Fighting to Help

(In the last story, a tornado hit Chris and Maria's house and tore off the roof! But no one was hurt, and everyone was thankful that God's angels had protected them. All the other Shoebox Kids were safe, too. But the church was damaged. Would their Shoebox Sabbath School room still be there?)

"Tell me all about it!" DeeDee said as she and Maria stood and talked beside the big truck in Maria's driveway. Her mom and dad, along with several other church members, were helping load the truck with the Vargases' furniture.

The girls went to the window and looked in. "We were hiding right there in that closet when it hit," Maria explained.

"Have you seen the church yet?" DeeDee asked.

"Dad says that after we get everything moved to our new apartment, we're going to the church to see what we can do there." Maria watched another car drive up as she spoke. It was Sammy and his grandfather.

As his grandfather went into the house, Sammy ran over to the girls. Maria told about the storm again.

Sammy nodded. "We were hiding in the basement at our house. But, Maria, where is your roof?"

Maria looked puzzled. "I told you. The tornado took it."

"I know that," Sammy said, "but where did it take it? All those boards and shingles and everything have to be somewhere."

Maria laughed. "We don't know. Dad said the fire department were looking for it all over town. Tornados sure do strange things. My mom had a vase of roses on the table there by the couch. After the tornado hit, the couch was still there, the vase was still there, even the rose stems were still there. But the rose petals were gone."

"Wow," Sammy said, "that's amazing. I wish I could have seen it."

Later that afternoon, many of the church members met at the church to see what could be done there. They gathered around Pastor Hill in the parking lot. "Please be very careful," he asked them. "There is broken glass everywhere. The rest of the sanctuary roof may still fall. We're asking everyone to stay out except for Mr. Teller and his crew."

Fighting to Help

As Pastor Hill passed out work assignments to the adults, the Shoebox Kids gathered together and whispered. "Does anyone know if our Shoebox is OK?" Sammy asked. Everyone shook their heads. "Well, my grandparents won't let me go inside. Can anyone else go in?" Everyone shook their heads again.

"Then we'll have to go around and . . ."

"Hi!" someone behind Sammy said. "What are you guys planning now?"

"Mrs. Shue! Are we glad to see you! Have you been to the Shoebox? Is it OK?" Everyone seemed to speak at the same time.

"Whoa, one question at a time," she laughed. "I've been so glad that God protected us all that I hadn't thought about the Shoebox. I hear that there was some damage on the back side of the church where the Shoebox is. Let's walk around the church and try to peek in the windows."

After everyone promised to watch for broken glass, they began their trip across the church yard. Chris got behind Willie to help push his wheelchair over the branches that were lying everywhere.

"Look at that!" Maria pointed to a large tree that had fallen over onto the lawnmower-storage building. "The lawnmower must be smashed."

"Which window is ours?" asked DeeDee as they walked nearer. "Is that it?" she asked, pointing to a broken window.

"No, it's the next one," Mrs. Shue said. "And look, it's not broken!" She went up close and peered inside. "Everything's still there; everything looks fine." She smiled as the kids cheered.

"Mrs. Shue, what's all this?" Jenny asked. "There are clothes all over back here. There are even some caught up in the trees."

"Oh, no," Mrs. Shue shook her head sadly. "Those are the clothes that were being collected for homeless people. The storm must have pulled them right out of the broken window in that room and scattered them across the yard."

"I know," Willie said excitedly, "let's pick them up. That's something the adults will let us do."

"I'll get some plastic bags," Mrs. Shue agreed. "Maybe you can have a contest to see who can pick up the most."

Soon they were ready. "Let's have two teams," Sammy suggested.

"It'll be the boys against the girls," DeeDee declared. Everyone nodded, so she said, "Ready, set, go!"

Soon, Shoebox Kids were running all over the ground like rabbits. Chris and Sammy were throwing clothes at Willie, who was stuffing them into bags. DeeDee and Maria tossed clothes to Jenny. For a few minutes, there was running and shouting and laughing as everyone had fun. But then the voices seemed to change.

"We're winning. We're faster than you."

"Hey, Chris, I had that shirt."

"I guess you guys are just too slow."

"I was climbing the tree to get that one, DeeDee."

"Too bad. I got it first."

Then it got worse. Chris dashed up and grabbed some of the clothes lying around Jenny and threw them to Willie. "Hey, that's not fair," Maria shouted. "We picked those up."

Chris just laughed. "They weren't in a bag, so we can pick them up."

"Oh, sure," DeeDee said, "Then I'll just get these." She opened one of the bags the boys had filled up and pulled out some clothes. "Here, Jenny, put these in our bag."

"Wait a minute," Chris shouted, "you can't do that." He rushed to grab the clothes back, and DeeDee held on to them. They were each pulling on a shirt, when it ripped almost in half.

"Stop it!" Jenny shouted. Everyone froze and stared at her. They had never heard her shout like that. "What are you fighting about? We're supposed to be here to help."

"Jenny's right," Willie said. "These are clothes for the homeless people, and we're fighting over picking them up. Aren't we supposed to be Jesus' hands, doing His work?"

Chris dropped the shirt and looked down at the ground. "I guess I forgot why we were here. I just wanted to win."

DeeDee slumped down to the ground. "I forgot, too. We're supposed to be here helping, and we're just fighting." Maria sat beside her and nodded.

"I'm sorry." Everyone seemed to say it at once, and they all laughed.

"Now," Jenny said, "let's just work together and pick up all the clothes we can find."

Later, when Mrs. Shue checked on them, she asked, "So who's winning?"

"All of us," Willie answered. "We decided to just all work together. It's more fun that way."

After Mrs. Shue was gone, Willie rolled over to pick some clothes out of the big tree that had fallen onto the lawnmower building. Just for a second, he thought he heard something strange. He listened closely, then called the others. "Hey, come over here." They all ran to the fallen tree, asking questions as they came. "Shhh! Listen. I thought I heard something."

They listened, and then they all heard it. From somewhere under that fallen tree, a scratchy voice whispered, "Help!"

(To be continued.)

QUESTIONS

1. Did you know that tornados do strange things? Ask your parents or teacher if they have heard any strange stories about tornadoes.

2. Have you seen kids arguing and fighting about who is better or faster? Or about winning a game or contest? Does everyone seem happy when they fight?

3. Can you think of a time when you helped someone get some work done quickly?

4. Did you know that helping someone else will always make you happy? It will! Especially if you are doing work for God.

CHAPTER

TERRIBLE THINGS HAPPEN TO JOB
Trapped Under a Tree!

God had a meeting with the angels in heaven. Satan came to the meeting too. "Where have you come from, Satan?" God asked.

"I've been walking around on the earth," Satan answered.

"Did you see My follower Job?" God asked. "Did you see how he loves Me and stays away from evil?"

Satan scowled. "Job only follows You because You bless him and protect him. If You take away the things he has, he will curse You to Your face."

God told Satan, "You may do what you wish to Job's things or his family. But you can't hurt him."

Now Job was a rich man with a big family. He had seven boys and three girls. In his fields there were 7,000 sheep, 3,000 camels, 1,000 oxen, and 500 donkeys. Job followed God faithfully and taught his children about God too.

Satan came down and attacked Job. Robbers stole his oxen and donkeys. Lightning killed all his sheep. The Babylonians stole his camels. Then a terrible wind storm knocked down the house where all of his children were having a party. They were all killed. And all this happened on the same day!

"Now let's see what Job will do," Satan said.

Job was shocked and sad. But he didn't curse God. He didn't blame God. He said, "God gives, and He takes away. Blessed be the name of the Lord."

There was another meeting in heaven. Satan was there again. "Did you see My faithful servant Job? After everything you did, he still follows Me."

"Of course he does," Satan said. "You're still protecting him. Let me attack his body, and he will curse You."

So God let Satan do what he wished to Job himself. Satan could hurt him, but he couldn't *kill* him.

So Satan made sores all over Job's body. Job was miserable. He hurt everywhere.

"Why don't you curse God and die?" his wife asked.

Three of Job's friends came to visit. "Job, this trouble has come because of some sin you have committed," they said.

But Job said, "I haven't sinned. I haven't done anything wrong."

No matter how bad he felt or what other people said, Job refused to curse God. But he did ask God why these terrible things were happening to him.

Finally God spoke to Job. He didn't argue with the ideas that the other people had given Job. He didn't even explain why good people sometimes suffer. He said, "Job, were you there when I created the world? Were you there when I put the clouds in the sky or the water in the ocean? Did you see Me create the sky or the mountains?" He told Job about His goodness, His power, and His wisdom.

Even though Job didn't get answers about the bad things that happened to him, he learned more about God. He learned that understanding *why* all the bad things had happened wasn't important. God was God, and He loved Job—*that* was what was important!

God healed Job's sores and pains and blessed him. Job lived for another 140 years. He ended up twice as rich as he was before. He had twice as many animals, and he even had seven more sons and three more daughters.

Job had proved to the whole universe that nothing—absolutely nothing, no matter how terrible—can overcome a person who knows that God loves him.

Trapped Under a Tree!

(In last week's story, the Shoebox Kids were picking up clothes that the tornado had scattered all over the back church yard. They learned that they could get more work done and be happier if they worked together. Then Willie heard a whisper from under a fallen tree. Was someone trapped?)

The Shoebox Kids were gathered around Willie at the fallen tree. "Shhh! Listen. I thought I heard a voice."

They listened, and then they all heard it. From somewhere under that fallen tree, a scratchy voice whispered, "Help!"

"Someone is under there! Whoever it is must have been in the lawnmower shed," Maria whispered.

"And whoever it is must be trapped and hurt," Sammy whispered. They all looked at each other.

"What do we do?" Chris asked.

Willie took a deep breath and shouted. "Are you hurt? Do you need help?"

The voice spoke again. "Willie? Willie, is that you?"

"Grandpa?" Willie leaned forward in his wheelchair. "Grandpa, is that you?" he asked.

"Willie," the voice spoke, "Willie, go get your dad. Go get some help."

Willie sat up. "Chris, run and find my dad, wherever he is. DeeDee and Maria, run and tell Mrs. Shue or Pastor Hill, or someone, to call an ambulance. Sammy and Jenny, help me try to move these branches. Maybe we can reach him. Grandpa, help is coming. Hang on."

DeeDee and Maria almost ran right into Mrs. Shue at the side of church. Quickly, they explained. "We need an ambulance."

Mrs. Shue didn't hesitate. "The church phones aren't working. Maria, isn't there a phone in your dad's car?"

"Yes! Let's find him." Maria led the way.

Chris ran right past his mother through the main doors of the church. "Chris, where are you going?"

"I can't explain right now, Mom," he shouted over his shoulder. He ran right up to the doors of the sanctuary, stuck his head in and shouted. "Mr. Teller! Where's Mr. Teller?"

"Hey, Chris, you can't be in here," Pastor Hill said. Then Mr. Teller stuck his head up from behind the pulpit.

Chris shouted. "Mr. Teller! Come quick! Willie's grandpa is trapped in the lawnmower shed under that big tree. Hurry!"

Mr. Teller dropped everything and ran out after Chris. Pastor Hill was right behind.

Trapped Under a Tree!

Sammy was pushing through branches, trying to reach the door of the smashed building. "I'll hold this branch back," Jenny said. "Try crawling under that big one."

"Grandpa, help is coming," Willie kept saying. Then he saw Chris and his dad. "Dad! Grandpa's under there," he cried.

"OK, Willie. We'll get him out. Dad! Are you OK? Are you near the door?" Willie's dad crawled closer toward the door as he spoke. Sammy and Jenny held back limbs and helped him through.

Maria and DeeDee ran up with Mrs. Shue. "The ambulance is on its way. The fire department rescue squad is coming, too," Mrs. Shue reported. "How is he?" she asked Willie.

"He was still talking to me," Willie said with tears in his eyes. "He sounded OK."

Willie's dad shouted back through the branches. "We need a saw to cut through these branches." Just then, Mr. Vargas arrived with a chain saw.

"I've got the saw. Kids, step back now." Chris stepped out of his dad's way and helped Mrs. Shue pull Willie's wheelchair back. They could hear the siren of the ambulance in the distance. The Shoebox Kids gathered around Willie and watched. "I guess there's nothing else we can do," DeeDee said softly.

"You've all done a lot already. You found him and brought help. Besides, there is something we can do. We can pray for Willie's grandpa." And they did.

Later that evening at the hospital, Willie wheeled into his grandpa's room. "Are you awake, Grandpa?"

"Is that you, Willie? Come on in here." He reached out

and grabbed Willie's hand. "I sure am glad you were there today. Thank you for finding me."

"What happened, Grandpa? How did you get trapped in the lawnmower shed?"

"Since your grandmother is off visiting your Aunt Margaret, I went out to eat. I was driving through the storm when I heard the tornado warning, so I stopped the car at the church. I thought I would wait there, just to be safe. But instead of staying inside, I decided to go around and check the gutters to be sure that the rain water would flow away."

Willie shook his head. "Why did you go into the shed?"

His grandpa laughed. "I heard the tornado coming. It sounded like a freight train. The lawnmower shed was the closest building, so I ran in there and slammed the door behind me. I lay down by the lawnmower and covered my head."

"Grandpa, were you afraid?"

"Yes, Willie, I was. But I prayed for God's protection, and I waited. I was fine until that tree fell. When it crashed through the roof, it hit the lawnmower instead of me. It fell across where I was, so I couldn't move. But I wasn't hurt. God was with me even there in the lawnmower shed. I prayed that God would send an angel to find me. And He did!"

Willie blushed. "Grandpa, I'm not an angel. But I'm sure glad I heard you whisper."

"Me, too, Willie. By today, I was so thirsty and dry I could hardly talk. But I'll be fine now. The doctors will send me home tomorrow. Thanks again, buddy. And thank your friends for me. I know they helped."

The next Sabbath, the members of the Mill Valley Church met in their fellowship hall. The Shoebox Kids met in the Shoebox. Mrs. Shue said, "We've all had an exciting week. But God watched over us, and we're safe. Willie, how is your grandpa?"

"He'll be fine. He wanted me to thank all of you guys."

Mrs. Shue nodded. "I'm very proud of you all. You acted very responsibly in that crisis. And I'm very thankful that you were working back there and heard his voice."

Willie raised his hand. "Mrs. Shue? Grandpa says that God used me as an angel to find him. And all of us worked together to rescue him. I guess we really were Jesus' hands this time."

QUESTIONS

1. Did you know that Jesus is always with you, even when something bad happens?

2. If you are ever scared or in danger, like Willie's grandpa was, can you be sure that Jesus will be there with you?

3. Has Jesus ever used you as one of His angels?

4. Did Jesus get to use you as His hands this quarter? He wants your help all summer, too!

If you enjoyed this book, don't miss the other
Shoebox Kids Bible Stories, by *Jerry D. Thomas.*

1. **Creation to Abraham.** Creation, the Sabbath, Cain and Abel, the Flood, Abraham and Isaac. Every chapter is a double story— one from the Bible, then a Shoebox story that applies the Bible lesson. Paper, 128 pages. 0-8163-1823-9.

2. **From Isaac to the Red Sea.** The Bible stories in this book start with Eliezer's search for a wife for Isaac, include Joseph's dreams, and end with the parting of the Red Sea and bread from heaven. Paper, 128 pages. 0-8163-1877-8.

3. **From the Ten Commandments to Jericho.** Water from the rock, the Ten Commandments, the golden calf, the brass serpent, Balaam's donkey, and crossing the Jordan. Paper, 128 pages. 0-8163-1911-1.

4. **From Joshua to David, Goliath, and Jonathan**. Joshua gets tricked by the Gibeonites, the day the sun stood still, Samson defeats the Philistines, and David battles Goliath. Paper, 128 pages. 0-8163-1949-9.

5. **From the Witch of Endor to Elisha the Prophet**. King Saul uses a witch to talk with Samuel's "ghost," Elijah takes a fiery chariot ride to heaven, and an army runs away from Elisha. Paper, 128 pages. 0-8163-1971-5.

Order from your ABC by calling **1-800-765-6955**, or get online and shop our virtual store at **www.AdventistBookCenter.com**.
- Read a chapter from your favorite book.
- Order online.
- Sign up for email notices on new products.